A DESOLATE CHRISTMAS

Victorian Romance

FAYE GODWIN

*Tica House
Publishing*

Sweet Romance that Delights and Enchants!

PERSONAL WORD FROM THE AUTHOR

Dearest Readers,

I'm so delighted that you have chosen one of my books to read. I am proud to be a part of the team of writers at Tica House Publishing. Our goal is to inspire, entertain, and give you many hours of reading pleasure. Your kind words and loving readership are deeply appreciated.

I would like to personally invite you to sign up for updates and to become part of our **Exclusive Reader Club**—it's completely Free to Join! I'd love to welcome you!

Much love,

Faye Godwin

VISIT HERE to Join our Reader's Club and to Receive Tica House Updates:

https://victorian.subscribemenow.com/

PART I

CHAPTER 1

Mama's eyes were the same shade of amber as her hair, except that the light scattered a little differently inside them. Staring up into them, Lena thought they were the same colour as her favourite milk chocolates. Maybe a little richer; and milk chocolate didn't make the candlelight come to life the way Mama's eyes did.

"Mama, you have such pretty eyes." Lena reached up with her hands, laying one on each of Mama's soft cheeks. "I love them."

Mama smiled. "I love your eyes too, Lena." She reached out to touch the tip of Lena's nose with an elegant forefinger. "They're the bluest of blues."

Lena giggled. "Your eyes look like chocolate."

Mama scooped Lena up into her arms, planting a kiss on her forehead as she sat down in the armchair by the little bed. Lena snuggled into her lap, placing her freshly washed head on Mama's shoulders. "How come some people have blue eyes and some people have brown eyes?" Lena asked, trying to hold back the wave of sleepiness that was threatening to over-whelm her.

"Well, it all depends what the fairies put in them," said Mama.

"So the fairies put chocolate in your eyes?" asked Lena in wonder.

"They must have." Mama nuzzled Lena's cheek, then kissed it.

"But what did they put in my eyes?"

Mama sat back in the armchair, thinking about the question. It was late, and the fire in the hearth was crackling warmly, filling the nursery with its dancing light. The gas lamps on the walls seemed bland by comparison. Lena listened to Mama's voice, gazing at the little rocking-horses that adorned the wallpaper of her room.

"I think the fairies went all the way up into the summer sky," said Mama. "They made a little fire out of their magic, and they melted a corner of the sky and put it in a teacup. Then they came to you when you were a baby and poured the pretty sky right into your eyes." Mama reached for Lena's hair, twirling one of her ringlets around her finger. "And while they were about it, they spun a few rays of sunshine into hair for you on a spinning wheel."

Lena giggled. "Tell me another story, Mama," she said.

"It's bedtime, my darling."

"Please, Mama? Pretty please," Lena begged. "It doesn't have to be a long one."

"Oh, all right, then." Mama cuddled her closer. "Do you want to hear another story about fairies?"

"No, not fairies." Lena pointed to the little book resting on the nightstand by her bed, right beside the fluffy white stuffed mouse she loved more than anything. "The story about the birdie."

"Ah, nothing new then, I see," said Mama with a gentle laugh that rocked Lena where she lay against her chest. "You do love this little birdie of yours, don't you?" She leaned forward to pick up the well-thumbed book and placed the mouse in Lena's lap. "All right, then, darling. Let's read the story about the birdie."

Lena leaned her head against Mama's shoulder, sucking on the mouse's left ear as Mama opened the book. The first page had a picture of a little brown bird perching on the very edge of a nest.

"Once upon a time, there was a little bird who lived in a cozy nest in the woods," Mama read. Her voice washed over Lena like warm, clear water. She turned the page. "The little bird lived with his mama and papa, and they loved one another very, very much."

"I like this picture," said Lena, touching it with a finger. The mama, papa and baby bird were all hugging each other in the nest. Lena liked how the papa bird's wings were wrapped around his little family.

"So do I," said Mama. She kissed Lena's cheek and turned the page. "One day, the little bird's mama and papa went out to find some seeds and berries for supper. The little bird sat on the edge of the nest, waiting for them to come home."

Lena cuddled closer to Mama. "This part is scary," she whispered.

Mama kept reading. "Suddenly, a big gust of wind came up out of nowhere. 'Oh, no!' cried the little bird. He tried to hold onto the nest with his tiny feet, but they were not strong enough. The wind swept him right up out of the nest and into the air."

"The poor little bird!" said Lena.

"When the wind stopped, the little bird was on the other side of the forest. He had never been so far away from his nest before, and he didn't know how to get back home. He was so afraid," Mama read.

Lena stared sadly at the picture of the little bird huddling on the ground. His eyes were frightened. "Read quickly, Mama," she pleaded. "I want him to get home."

"The little bird knew that he had to get back to his nest. He thought he knew which way it was, so he started to hop along the ground, because he could not yet fly. But oh, no! Who is this?" Mama turned the page, and Lena squealed at the picture.

"It's the big bad wolf!" she cried.

"It's the big bad wolf!" Mama read. "The little bird was so frightened. He began to hop faster and faster, but the wolf was chasing him. 'What can I do?' the little bird cried. 'How can I escape?'"

"Fly, little bird," Lena whispered.

"As the wolf came closer and closer, the little bird flapped and flapped his wings. And then, when the wolf was almost upon him, he jumped up – and he began to fly." Mama smiled. "He flew all the way up over the forest, and he saw the most amazing view."

Lena admired the picture spread across the next page. The little bird wore a wide smile on his beak, his wings stretched out wide.

"Then, the little bird saw his nest waiting for him across the forest. He spread out his wings and flew all the way home in a jiffy," said Mama. "He settled back down into his nest and said to himself..."

Lena joined in with her mother, parroting the last line. "The world is very beautiful, but flying is for going home."

"The end," said Mama, kissing the top of Lena's head.

Lena yawned. Mama laughed, scooping her up. Lena allowed herself to be lowered into her bed and she lay on the pillow, eyes closed, as Mama gently tucked the blankets up around her.

"One day, I want to fly just like the little bird," she whispered.

Mama kissed her forehead. "As long as you always fly home, my darling," she whispered as Lena drifted slowly off to sleep.

THE DOORKNOB THAT ELLA WAS POLISHING ALREADY SHONE like a mirror in full sunlight but judging by the conversation going on inside the master's parlour, she definitely wasn't done with buffing it. Working her cloth back and forth over the knob, she leaned a little closer to the keyhole. The voices from inside were faint, but Ella was a master eavesdropper.

"... very good references." The voice belonged to Master Charles, and Ella pulled a face. She hated him passionately; he seemed absolutely immune to all of the charms she had turned on in a bid to get some favouritism out of him. "She's young, but she comes from a respectable family and has had a good education."

"Well, Charles, youth isn't a crime, you know." Ella's mistress, Joan Phillips, gave a gentle laugh.

"Oh, I know, darling." There was a smile in Charles' voice. Ella rolled her eyes, knowing that the couple were probably staring into one another's eyes again with the ridiculous sappiness that they utterly failed to confine to the bedroom. Sitting at meals, walking through the home, traveling – it didn't matter the situation; Joan and Charles always looked at one another like nobody else existed. "But I do want nothing but the best for our precious little Lena."

"I know you do, love," said Joan. "So do I. That's why we're going to hire a wonderful governess to start her education. You've done so much research, Charles, that I know this young lady will be perfect. What did you say her name was?"

"Miss Goodman," said Charles. "Sally Goodman."

"Excellent. Let's have her for an interview," said Joan, "and let her meet Lena. We do have to discuss her wages."

"Of course, my dear. Now, you must tell me if you disagree, but I believe that a good governess is worth a good wage," said Charles.

Ella had completely forgotten about the doorknob. She leaned against the door, ear to the keyhole, and listened with all her might.

"I was thinking that fifty pounds a year would be fair," said Charles.

"Yes, darling. That sounds excellent," said Joan.

Ella could listen no more. She seized her rag and tin of polish and straightened up, striding off down the corridor, seething. "Fifty pounds a year!" she muttered to herself. "Those hateful dogs! If they can pay a *governess* fifty pounds a year, surely they can give me more than the measly twenty pounds I somehow have to make do with." She snorted as she hurried down the stairs to the kitchen. "Twenty pounds! But of course, I'm just a lowly parlour maid. Nobody thinks of *me*."

Still muttering, Ella barged into the kitchen. Almost at once, the housekeeper, Mrs. Phips, turned to her with a deep frown on her face.

"Ella!" she thundered. "Where have you been? I sent you off to polish the doorknobs hours ago."

"I've been polishing, ma'am," said Ella.

"I highly doubt it," said Mrs. Phips. "Don't tell me you've been up to no good again."

Ella opened a cupboard and tossed her rag and polish carelessly inside. "No good? Me? Never," she said.

"Ha!" Jerry, the footman, barked from the kitchen hearth, where he was warming his cold hands. "Polishing doorknobs? No wonder it took you so long. Have you been eavesdropping again, girl?"

"Oh, you know me," said Ella. "I never eavesdrop."

"Not at all," said Jerry sarcastically. "Not even that time when you heard Harold telling Penny about his brother's gambling problem and then got him fired because of it."

Ella shrugged. "Harold had it coming to him," she snapped.

"That's as may be, but what about his wife and children?" Mrs. Phips shook her head. "Honestly, Ella, why the master hasn't sent you packing already is quite beyond me."

"Because I'm a good parlour-maid, that's why." Ella seized a bucket and mop.

"There's no cause to be so disagreeable," said Jerry.

"I don't know what you're talking about." Ella tossed her head in a proud gesture. "I'm just doing what needs to be done to survive – and I suggest the rest of you start doing the same."

"Now, why would we want to do that?" said Mrs. Phips. "The master has always been kind to us."

"Oh, if you only knew what I know..." Ella tapped the side of her nose.

Mrs. Phips turned away, shaking her head, and Jerry snorted. But the little scullery-maid, Meg, who was on her knees scrubbing the floor, looked up at Ella with wide eyes. "What do you know, Ella?" she asked.

Ella leaned against the wall. "Oh, just a little piece of information about the master's affairs," she said. "One that's going to cause all of us to get pay cuts – or worse."

"What are you talking about?" demanded Mrs. Phips. "Business has never been better for the master."

"Ah, see, that's what he thinks, too," said Ella. "But he's about to hire some governess named Sally – Sally Goodman. And see, I've heard word on the street about Sally. It's nothing good."

"Nonsense," snorted Mrs. Phips. "You're just telling stories again, Ella."

"Why is it not good?" asked the wide-eyed Meg. "What did she do wrong?"

"Everyone says something different," said Ella ominously. "Some say she's a liar. Some say she's a plain petty thief. And some say she's a seducer, going to drive a wedge between the master and the mistress."

"Rubbish," said Jerry. "They'll never let that happen." But there was a note of doubt in his tone.

Ella heard that doubt and pounced on it. "And worst of all," she went on, "the master is practically bankrupting himself with what he's going to pay her."

"How much is it?" asked Meg.

Ella smirked. "Seventy pounds a year."

"Seventy pounds!" The housekeeper almost dropped the pot of food she was lifting off the stove. "That's codswallop. That's the same as I'm paid."

"It's the honest truth, I'm telling you," said Ella. "I'm surprised, really. With Sally's reputation, I wouldn't let her into my house even as a scullery-maid."

"Oh, Ella," said Jerry. "Go away and spread your nonsense somewhere else."

But there it was again: that gleam of doubt in his eye. Ella slouched off, trying to hide her triumphant smirk. Meg believed every word she was ever told, and she was sure to spread the rumour all through the servants' quarters like wildfire.

By the time Sally Goodman arrived, she wouldn't have a friend in the world. Not one, except for Ella Brown.

CHAPTER 2

"He spread out his wings and flew all the way home in a jiffy." Sally Goodman tucked some of her pale hair back behind her ear. "He settled back down into his nest…"

"… and said to himself, 'The world is very beautiful, but flying is for going home'," said Lena, clapping her hands in glee.

Sally laughed, closing the book and putting it aside. "Well, aren't you a clever little thing, Lena?" she said, reaching for Lena's hands. "You know that book inside out."

"It's my favourite," said Lena, looking up at Sally.

"Well, then we'll be sure to read it often." Sally smiled. "But now, we really do have to go back to learning about shapes."

"I don't like shapes," Lena complained as Sally reached for the basket of wooden blocks. "They're so boring."

"Well, we do have to learn about them, Lena," said Sally. She took a blue block out of the basket. "Now, be a clever girl and tell me what shape this is."

Lena shrugged. "A square?"

"No, darling. Remember, a square has sides all the same length."

Lena knew that she didn't have to try too hard, not with Sally. She looked a little closer. "A triangle?" she said, knowing it wasn't.

"Almost," said Sally encouragingly. "It's a rectangle." She reached for another block. "Now..."

"No," said Lena cheerfully. "No more shapes!" She grabbed her mouse. "Let's build a house for Mr. Mousie out of the blocks instead."

"Lena..." Sally began.

"Please, Sally?" Lena gazed up at Sally in just the right way. "Pretty, pretty please?"

Sally smiled. Lena loved Sally's smile; it was so warm and gentle. "Oh, all right," she said, laughing. "Let's build Mr. Mousie a little housie, shall we?"

"Yay!" Lena giggled. She clambered up onto Sally's lap, clutching the mouse's tail in one chubby fist, and put her arms around her governess's neck. "I love you, Sally."

Sally gave a little laugh of surprise, returning Lena's hug. "Well, I love you too, little Lena," she said.

"I was so scared when Papa first told me I was going to get a goveyness," Lena said, gazing up at Sally's soft eyes.

"You mean a governess." Sally kissed the top of Lena's head.

"A governess," said Lena.

"Why were you scared, little darling?" asked Sally, cradling Lena in her arms.

"Well, I didn't know anyone except Mama and Papa and Granny and Auntie Joy and Uncle Ben, and Uncle Ben is scary," said Lena. "And Ella and Mrs. Phips. So I thought maybe you would be scary, like Uncle Ben."

"And am I scary?" asked Sally, her voice on the brink of laughter.

Lena giggled. "No, you're not scary."

"Not even a little bit?" Sally raised an eyebrow.

"Not even a tiny little bit."

"Not even when I do this?" Propping Lena on her lap, Sally made her two hands into claws and growled.

Lena giggled. "Not at all."

"What about this?" Sally gave another growl and then started tickling Lena's tummy. Lena laughed until she screamed.

"No! Stop!" she squealed. "Stop!"

Sally laughed, putting Lena down on the floor. "Well, I'm glad you don't think I'm scary then, darling."

"Not one bit," said Lena, hugging Sally's knees. "I like being with you."

Sally gazed down at her, a gentle smile tugging at her thin, pale lips. "I like being with you, too," she said, touching Lena's nose.

Lena giggled. She'd thought that life couldn't get any better with Mama and Papa both loving her so much, but now that she had Sally, she knew everything was even better.

⚜

ELLA WAS WALKING TOO FAST. DIRTY WATER SLOPPED OUT of the bucket she carried, drops of it splashing onto the pristine carpet. That was going to be a lot of work for some hapless housemaid to scrub out, she noted with just a little satisfaction. That would show that snippy little Mindy how to behave around her elders and betters.

"Complaining that I'm treating her wrong, my foot!" Ella muttered angrily. "And Mrs. Phips only listening because she has it in for me – like everyone else." She gave a frustrated sigh. "What have I ever done to this world to make it hate me so much?"

She paused at the door to the nursery, listening begrudgingly. Mistress Joan had given her strict instructions only to clean the nursery during Lena's nap time, "to avoid distracting the little one from her lessons". Ella knew full well that the fancy woman thought she'd be a bad influence on the spoiled little brat. Not hearing the little girl's laughter, Ella opened the door and stepped inside.

The nursery was bigger than three or four of the servants' rooms put together. A huge, luxurious fireplace was filled with warmth and golden light; there were toys strewn across the brightly patterned hearth rug, a gigantic bookshelf filled with colourful books, and a cot in the corner in which Lena was just a mop of golden curls covered with her fleece blanket. The thick, royal blue curtains framing the window made the snowflakes tumbling down outside look picturesque instead of deathly cold. Ella sighed, planting the bucket down on the floor with a thump. Lena didn't stir, but there was a movement from the armchair by the fire, and a pale face framed by white-blonde hair gazed up at Ella.

"Oh," said Ella, slightly startled. "I didn't see you there."

The governess quickly wiped at her eyes, which were red with tears. "Sorry," she said. "I'd get out of your way, but I'm not allowed to leave Lena while she's sleeping." She sniffed, dabbing at her nose with a handkerchief.

Ella saw golden opportunity in the governess's tears. "It's Goodman, isn't it?" she said, putting on her friendliest voice as she went over to where the governess sat. "Miss Goodman?"

The young woman sniffed. "Sally, please," she said.

"Well, it's nice to meet you, Sally." Ella put a hand on her shoulder. "I'm Ella."

Sally looked up at her, surprise in her eyes. "You... you're the first person to introduce yourself to me," she said.

"Really?" said Ella, feigning shock. A note of triumph rang in the back of her mind; the stories she'd told Mrs. Phips and the others had clearly worked to make them shun the newcomer.

"Yes." Sally wiped her eyes dry with the handkerchief. "I don't know why I told you that. Do excuse me." She sniffed. "I know this is most unbecoming."

She sounded good and educated.

"Not at all, dear," said Ella in her best motherly tone. "You look so upset. Can I get you anything? Have you had something to eat yet?"

"Y-yes, I have." Sally gestured to the lonely lunch on the little table beside the armchair.

"It can't be nice, eating all by yourself," said Ella. "Well, it isn't nice — I know that much. I have to sit by myself in my quarters, too. The rest of the staff are just awful to me."

"They are?" Sally stared at her.

"Yes — they're dreadful! I don't know why," said Ella.

"They've been avoiding me, too." Sally's voice broke slightly. "I don't understand it. I know many governesses think they're better than the servants, but I just want to be friends. Yet even the housekeeper has been giving me the cold shoulder, although I've seen her being kind to the kitchen maids."

"Oh, that kindness is just put on," said Ella quickly. "Mrs. Phips is a cruel old bag sometimes. Before I became a parlour-maid, she used to lock me up in a closet or cane my hands for making the tiniest mistake in the scullery."

"How awful!" exclaimed Sally. "Why would she do such a thing?"

"There's no understanding some people, dear," said Ella sagely. She patted Sally's shoulder. "Keep your chin up, now. They'll most likely always be cruel to you, but you don't have to let that get you down."

Sally looked up at her. "Why are you being so kind to me?"

"We've got nothing in this life except each other," said Ella. "Being cruel doesn't do any good, does it, then?"

"I suppose not." Sally sighed. "Although it's all that I've ever known."

Ella cheered inwardly. She'd gained this weak-willed little governess's trust — and there were many things that she could do with that trust. Knowing that she'd be fired if she was seen, she perched on the edge of the nearest armchair. "How so, love?" she said. "Why would anyone want to be cruel to a pretty little thing like you?"

"I don't know," said Sally, a fresh bout of tears running down her cheeks. "I grew up in such a nice little middle-class home. My papa is a tailor, and my mama is a nurse. I had six siblings, and I suppose I was just the quietest of them all. Somehow, I always ended up being pushed aside."

"That's terrible," said Ella.

"My parents were always cold with me. Papa believed it would make me grow a backbone," said Sally. "That's why they made me get this job as a governess, thinking that I was just being stubborn when I kept turning down every suitor that they found for me. Little did they know..." She stopped.

"Little did they know what, dear?" asked Ella, laying a maternal hand on Sally's arm.

"Well, I shouldn't say," said Sally, her cheeks colouring. "It's shameful, really. The mistress would be so furious if she found out – I'd be dismissed at once. I-I don't even know why I'm blathering on to you. We hardly know one another."

Ella sensed an opportunity for leverage. She put on her warmest smile. "Now, now, dear. You can tell old Ella," she said. "These kind of secrets are a heavy burden to bear alone. You need to confide in someone, or they'll eat you up."

Sally looked up, her eyes shining with loneliness and vulnerability. "It's... it's a man," she said.

It always is, Ella thought. "Oh?"

"We met at a dinner," said Sally. "It was a few years ago, and I was just seventeen. He was so kind and polite. He listened to everything I was saying... which my family never did. All they wanted was to tell me what to do, but he..." She sighed, a hint of wistfulness creeping into her expression. "He was just so kind. So... interested."

"But your parents didn't want him to court you?" Ella guessed.

"No... no. My parents don't even know that we've been seeing each other for years." Sally's eyes filled with tears once more. "Oh, Ella, it's so shameful to say it out loud, but he has been so terribly kind to me. The only person who's ever been kind to me."

"What is it?" asked Ella, trying to hide her eagerness.

"He's married," Sally croaked. "He's married to another woman. But she doesn't love him. She's an old nag, and she hates him, and he was just... just looking for love, like I was." Sally sniffed hard. "It has to be a secret, of course. I can't tell my family. They would hate me."

Ella almost clapped her hands in glee. She couldn't have asked for a juicier little nugget of information than this. Patting Sally's shoulder, she made consoling noises. "There, there, darling," she said. "Don't you worry, duck. Your secret's safe with me."

"Oh, thank you, Ella." Sally sighed, clutching at Ella's hands. "You've been so terribly kind. It feels so good to have someone to talk to."

"Anytime, darling," said Ella. She smiled, feeling golden opportunity in the air. "Anytime."

CHAPTER 3

The snowflakes looked like bits of magic, or perhaps music notes turned into something physical. Lena could hear the gentle trickle of notes pouring out of the house nearby as their neighbour's daughter practiced a carol on the harpsichord. She recognized one of the Christmas songs her mama had sung to her last year, the only Christmas she could remember. The words eluded her, but she knew the tune was familiar, playful, just like the snowflakes that were filtering down out of the sky. Each one of them was precious and unique, like a music note, and their fluttering harmony as they settled on every surface was a quiet hymn to the beauty of winter.

Lena laughed as a snowflake settled on her cheek like an icy kiss. She held out her hands in wonder, watching them settle on the sleeves of her favourite pink dress. They melted where they struck the palms of her small hands, but they remained on the dress, a little layer of powdered music coating the fabric. She took a step forward, enjoying the way the snow crunched underneath her little shoes.

"Sally," she cried, turning around. "Look at my footprints!"

Sally startled at the sound of Lena's voice, as if she'd forgotten that she was there at all. She straightened on the garden bench, staring at her. "What?"

"Look!" Lena pointed at her perfect little footprints in the snow. "Aren't they pretty? Come and make footprints with me, Sally."

"Oh, no, no, darling." Sally glanced up at the sky, then across the snowy lawn, bordered by snow-dusted trees that looked like they'd been taken straight from the cover of a Christmas card. "The snow is falling fast. You and I should go inside."

"Just some more minutes, Sally," Lena begged. She crunched over to her governess, gripping her skirt in both hands. "Why won't you come and play with me? Let's draw in the snow like we did yesterday."

"Not today, darling," said Sally. She dabbed at her eyes, and Lena noticed that they looked red and more watery than ever.

"Why won't you play with me today?" Lena asked, clambering up onto the bench and cuddling up to Sally's side as she gazed up at her.

"It's just not a good day, dear," said Sally. "Come on. Let's go inside."

Lena gripped her hand, noticing that Sally's eyes looked as if the colour had been washed straight out of them — just like Mr. Mousie's bow tie. It had been red once, when Lena was little, but now it was sort of pink. Mama said it was from all the washing.

"What's the matter, Sally?" she asked, feeling a wave of sorrow at her governess's tears. "You look so sad. Are you sad?"

"A little," Sally admitted, her eyes filling with tears. She looked away, dabbing at her eyes again with her handkerchief.

"Why?" asked Lena, climbing into Sally's lap and putting her arms around her neck. "Let me hug it better." She cuddled her head against Sally's chest.

Sally gave a broken little laugh, resting her hand against Lena's back. "Oh, Lena," she said. "I don't think you can hug it better this time."

"Why not?" Lena asked.

"I..." Sally looked away. "I think I might be in trouble," she said quietly.

"I been in trouble before," said Lena. "I was naughty and talked back to my mama, and then I was in very big trouble." She smiled, laying a small hand on Sally's cheek. "But you don't have to be worried, Sally. Mama says that when I'm in trouble, it's not because she's mean. It's just because she loves me and wants me to learn the right things. It'll only be for a little while, you'll see. Just until you learn."

"Oh, Lena." Sally tried to smile. "It's not that."

"What is it?" asked Lena.

"I..." Sally sighed. She gently lifted Lena to the floor and got up, taking her hand. "Come on. Let's go inside."

Before Lena could argue, Sally started to stride decisively back toward the house. Lena skipped alongside to keep up.

"Is it because you miss Mama and Papa?" asked Lena. "I miss them too, very very much. I know Mama said that they had to go away for business, but I can't wait for them to get back. I hope they'll be home for Christmas."

"They will be, Lena," said Sally quietly. "Don't worry."

"Then we'll all have Christmas together – you and me and Mama and Papa," said Lena, beaming. "Come on, Sally – smile. It'll be fun. We'll eat wonderful Christmas cake, and we'll decorate the whole house, and then we'll even have presents. It'll be wonderful."

Sally gave a gentle sigh, a tiny smile tugging at the corners of her lips. She scooped Lena up into her arms and settled her on her hip. "I hope so, sweetheart," she said. "I really do."

CHAPTER 4

Ella could hear Mrs. Phips shouting her name, and it gave her a sense of quiet satisfaction. She settled back into her sunny corner by the bins, stretching out her legs and enjoying the balmy winter sun. It was a lovely day to be doing nothing, rather than scrubbing things in the house – like she was probably supposed to be doing. But Mrs. Phips had never found her here in her hidden little nook. Sure, it was a little smelly with the bins all around, but at least it was nice and peaceful.

She leaned back, propping her back against the wall, and held back a yawn. It was time for her usual mid-morning nap, if she could hold back all the bad memories that threatened to swamp her anytime she took a moment's relaxation. Closing her eyes, Ella tried to think of something else – like dinner, or how she was going to find a way under Sally's guard to find out more...

"Ella!"

Ella opened her eyes. This time, it wasn't Mrs. Phips. She sat up, looking around. Sally's voice sounded distraught. She was calling from somewhere in the vegetable garden, so Ella rolled quickly onto her hands and knees, crept out from behind the bins well out of sight of the main house, and popped back up again by the wall separating the smelly little courtyard from the garden.

"Ella?" Sally called again, almost in a whisper. She sniffed, and Ella could hear she'd been crying.

Making her way quickly around the corner to the garden gate, Ella peered into the vegetable patch. Sally was standing by the bare, iced ground, wiping at her eyes with her handkerchief.

"Sally?" she called out.

"Oh! There you are." Sally's shoulders sagged with relief. Her eyes were raw. "I've been looking all over the house for you. I was just about to give up when I guessed you might be here." She looked around at the bare garden. "Although I don't know what you might be doing out here at this time of year."

"I was just taking out the rubbish," said Ella, lazily. She knew that Sally wouldn't suspect her of anything. "Why were you looking for me?" She reached for Sally's hand. "You look so upset. Is there something the matter?"

"Yes... yes, there is." Sally sniffed hard, a fresh wave of tears coursing down her pale cheeks. "There's something terribly the matter, Ella." Her voice grew hushed, and she looked around nervously.

"Come," said Ella, taking Sally's elbow. "Let's go somewhere more private." She led the crying girl into the empty greenhouse. Bugs scuttled away from their feet as she stepped inside and closed the door behind them. Sally shuddered visibly at the dirt around her, but she seemed too upset to care too much.

"Now," said Ella, "you can speak freely, dear. Tell me what it is that's gotten you so upset." She laid a gentle hand on Sally's shoulder.

"Oh, Ella, I'm almost too afraid to say it," said Sally.

"You know you can tell your Ella anything," said Ella comfortingly. "Haven't I been a good friend to you ever since you came here? Haven't we had such lovely conversations by the fire of an evening when you've been lonely?"

Sally swallowed, seeming to gain a little strength from Ella's words. "Yes," she said. "Yes, we have. You've been so good to me, Ella. I know I can trust you."

"There, there, now, dear," said Ella. "Tell me what it is."

"It's..." Sally swallowed, laying a hand on her skinny abdomen. "Ella," she whispered. "I'm with child."

A jolt of something that ran deeper than opportunism shot down Ella's spine. Her heart had been cold for years, but she suddenly felt a rush of horror at Sally's words. A memory flitted through her mind – one of her own bulging midriff, glancing down at it in love and pride. Gazing up at the eyes of the man opposite her, seeing his excitement. Not knowing, then, how quickly it was going to turn to revulsion and hatred.

"Sally, you poor thing!" The words popped out of Ella's mouth unbidden. She struggled to get back her composure, to find her cool, calculated thoughts again. "Is it..." she began.

"Yes," said Sally. "It's his. It's David's." She began to sob quietly, covering her face with her hands. "Oh, Ella, I tried so hard to be careful. But it was all for nothing."

"Are you sure?" Ella asked, taking a couple of deep breaths to dispel the dark memory in her mind.

"Yes, I'm sure. It can only be him... and I'm definitely pregnant." Sally looked up at Ella, her eyes swimming. "Oh, Ella, what am I going to do?"

"Does he know?"

"No. Not yet," said Sally.

"Good. Don't tell him," said Ella. "There's nothing but grief waiting for you if you do that."

"Why?" Sally's eyes filled with confusion.

"Trust me, Sally. Just don't tell him," said Ella. She took a deep breath. *You have to use this for survival, Ella,* she reminded herself. *Remember how your heart has betrayed you. Don't let it get involved.* "And you can't tell your family, either," she added.

"I know." Sally gave a whimper of fear. "If they find out, then they're going to throw me out of the house, Ella. They'll never forgive me. I'll end up in a workhouse. I can't go to a work-house – I'd never survive."

Looking at the girl's slight frame, Ella knew she was right. "So, there's nowhere you can go?"

"I..." Sally paused. "There is someone. My dear friend – she might be able to help me. She lives across London, and I haven't seen her in years, but she has a good heart. She's the only person in the world who might care. But I can't get away to go and see her, Ella. Not with Lena. I have to watch her all the time."

There! Ella grinned, knowing she'd stumbled straight into her opportunity. "Well, why don't you let me watch her?" she asked.

"You?" Sally paused. "What would the mistress say?"

"She's in India," Ella pointed out. "She'd never know. Let me watch the little girl for the afternoon while you get some time to sort out your mess. Nobody needs to know."

"Oh, Ella, you are a wonder," said Sally. "Thank you."

Ella waited for the magic words, knowing they were about to come.

"Of course, Sally," she said, with all the kindness she could muster. "Whatever you need."

"Ella, you're an angel." Sally gave Ella a quick hug. "How could I ever repay you?"

There they are. Ella put on her most humble expression, touching Sally's arm. "Well, dear, I won't be able to hide much from Mrs. Phips," she said. "I'll tell her that I fell asleep cleaning the nursery, but of course, I'll be punished and have to work late. I'll need to go out and buy some cordial to keep my strength up, but I can't afford it. We parlour-maids get paid a pittance, you know."

"Whatever you need, Ella," said Sally gratefully. "I'll give you whatever you need. Thank you so much."

Ella hid her smirk behind a kindly smile. "Of course," she said. "Anything for a friend."

❧

"Lena. Lena, darling. It's time for you to wake up."

Lena stretched her arms out to the side, blinking. Her cot was deliciously warm, and she could hear the fire crackling, filling the nursery with warmth and light. Blinking, she looked up at Sally. Her eyes were still red, but at least now they were dry. Reaching up, Lena brushed her fingertips across Sally's cheek.

"Do you feel better, dear Sally?" she whispered.

Sally gave her a fragile smile. "I do, thank you, darling," she said.

Lena sat up and stretched. "Good!" she said. "Can we play outside again this afternoon?"

"It's much too cold, dear," said Sally. "You're going to stay safely in the nursery and play with your toys, understand?"

Lena sat on the edge of the bed, and Sally knelt to put on her shoes. "Will you rock me on my rocking-horse?" she said hopefully.

"I will, but tomorrow," said Sally. "For this afternoon, Ella is going to look after you."

Lena frowned. "Who's Ella?"

"Ella is a very nice lady who also works for your parents." Sally didn't look up as she spoke, quickly tying one of Lena's shoelaces. "She's just going to keep an eye on you until I get back tomorrow morning."

"Where are you going?" asked Lena.

"I'm going..." Sally paused. "I'm going to get myself out of trouble," she said. "Now, you're going to be a very good girl and listen to Ella, all right?"

Lena nodded, brightening up. "Will Ella read to me?" she asked.

"Maybe, if you ask her very, very nicely," said Sally. "Ella is nice. You're going to have a lovely time with her."

Lena giggled. "All right," she said. "I can't wait to tell Mama all about it when she gets back."

"No!" said Sally, sharply.

Lena pulled back, shocked. Sally never spoke to her in that way – no one ever spoke to her in that way. She felt a ripple of fear at the look in Sally's eyes, and tears prickled at the back of her throat. "Wh-why are you angry with me?" she stammered.

"Oh, Lena, I'm sorry." Sally gripped Lena's shoulders gently. "I'm not angry with you. I'm just..." She paused.

"Hungry?" Lena guessed, instantly reassured.

"What?" Sally frowned.

"Are you hungry?" said Lena. "Mama says I'm very cranky when I'm hungry. Maybe that's why you're feeling cranky, Sally."

Sally laughed. "Maybe," she said, touching Lena's nose with the tip of her forefinger. "Now, darling, you must listen very closely. Ella looking after you is just our secret, all right? You can't tell your mama or papa." Sally winked. "It's a little secret just between the two of us, because you're my best friend, aren't you?"

Lena giggled. "I never had a secret before," she said. "Secrets sound like fun."

"I'm glad you think so." Sally kissed Lena's forehead. "Now, you'll be a good girl for Ella, won't you?"

"I'll be a very good girl," said Lena solemnly. "But I'll miss you."

"I'll be back before you know it." Sally straightened up. "See you soon, sweetheart."

She minced over to the door and pulled it open. Lena could just hear her muffled voice. "Are you sure you'll be all right with her?" Sally whispered. "She's a sweet little thing."

"Oh, of course," said another voice breezily. "Don't you worry. See you tomorrow."

"All right. Just... keep a good eye on her, all right?" Sally said. "She's the apple of the mistress's eye. And of my own, if I'm honest."

"Stop worrying." The voice was cheerful. "Off you go."

Sally left, and the lady who stepped into the room next was nothing like her at all. Where Sally was tall and slender and pale, this lady was short and squat. She had a mole on her cheek and dark brown hair that was roughly pulled back into a bun and squashed down under a grubby off-white bonnet. When she gave Lena a grin, one of her front teeth was missing.

"Hello, little missy," she said.

"Are you Ella?" asked Lena meekly.

"I am," said Ella. "And you're going to be a good girl this afternoon, do you hear?" She went over the nearest armchair by the fire and plopped noisily down into it.

"That's Mama's chair," said Lena.

"And that's your cot," said Ella, "and you can sit there on it without making a single peep all afternoon." She settled down into the armchair, interlacing her fingers over her belly.

Lena didn't move. "Aren't you going to play with me?" she asked. "Or read to me?"

Ella grunted. "No," she said. "Now quiet. You're interrupting my beauty sleep."

Lena sat very still in consternation. Ella wasn't nice at all – not like Sally had said. But poor Sally had looked so frightened and sad. For Sally's sake, Lena had to be a good girl.

Even if it looked like being a good girl meant a very long and very, very boring afternoon.

CHAPTER 5

Ella had to thump hard on the door to make herself heard over the loud laughter inside. "Hey!" she shouted, hammering again. "It's me. Your sister!"

"Just be patient!" a masculine voice shouted back. Ella recognized the voice of her eldest brother, Pete. She gave a snort of irritation and knocked again. This time, the door was yanked open.

"What do you want?" Pete demanded. His shirt was unbuttoned halfway down his chest, and he gave her a loose-lipped leer that spoke of the numerous beers that must already be sloshing around in his pudgy belly.

"Hello to you too, brother," said Ella. "It's my afternoon off. I thought I'd spend it with family."

"Why didn't you go to Ma's place, then?" demanded her younger brother, Fred. He was as stringy and gawky as Pete was soft and round.

"Because Ma hates me," Ella reminded them. "Are you going to let me in or not?"

"Or because you want to borrow money," said Pete suspiciously.

"Now why would I want to do that?" Ella grinned, taking her wallet out of her pocket and shaking it so that they could hear the jingle of coins within. "I've got more than enough."

Gary, Ella's middle brother, swiped at the wallet. Ella quickly returned it to her pocket. "Where did you get that from, sis?" he asked.

"I'll tell you if you let me in and give me a pint, how about that?" said Ella.

Begrudgingly, Pete pulled the door all the way open. "Come on in, then, I guess," he said. "Gary, get her what she asked for."

"Do I look like a barman to you?" grumbled Gary.

Ella tried not to look too closely as she walked into the grubby tenement that her three brothers had shared since they became adults. "Ugh, this place is just revolting," she said, pushing a couple of old beer bottles off the nearest chair and sitting down. "One of you lot should get married."

"We haven't had much luck in that department," said Fred, sitting down opposite her.

"I wonder why, three charmers like you," said Ella.

"What's that supposed to mean?" Fred demanded, resting his beer bottle on his belly as he lowered himself into a chair.

"She thinks we're beneath her just because we don't have a job in a fancy old house like her," sneered Gary. He planted a bottle down in front of her. "As if we want to be pushed around by some goody-two-shoes mistress."

"You don't know who's doing the pushing around, Gary," said Ella. She took a triumphant swig of the beer. "That mistress might think that she's got me under control, but the truth is, I've got her wrapped right around my little pinky." She grinned, holding it up. "I'm the one who's in charge around there."

Pete snorted. "I doubt it."

"It's true," said Ella. "How else do you think I've gotten hold of this money?"

"Well, we don't know, do we?" said Fred testily. "You haven't told us."

"All right, then, I'll tell you," said Ella.

Leaning back in her chair, she laid out her master plan to them, determined to impress her brothers. She told them everything: how she'd persuaded the staff that Sally was to be avoided long before the governess even showed her face in the manor, how she'd gotten Sally to trust her, and then how she'd found a weakness and exploited it for the extra cash.

"A pound she's given me, each of the three times I've had to watch that little mite for her," she said, grinning. "And all I do to earn that pound is lean back in a cushy armchair by the fire. She's not hardly any trouble at all."

"We've taught you well, sis," said Fred, with begrudging admiration.

Pete gave a deep-throated belly laugh. "We have. Just as conniving as her old man and her brothers, she is. A good little thief just like the rest of us."

Ella preened, enjoying the praise. But Gary wasn't smiling. Instead, when he leaned forward, elbows on the table, the look in his eyes was familiar: it was calculating.

"How old is the child?" he asked.

"I don't know," said Ella. "Four, maybe? Five? Six?"

"Still small enough." Gary looked over at his brothers, and the same expression came into their eyes.

Pete put his beer down on the table. "And you say she's quiet?"

"As a mouse," said Ella. "She's no trouble at all. Hardly makes a peep all afternoon."

"Is she pretty?" asked Fred.

Ella was slightly taken aback by the barrage of questions. "Why all the questions?" she asked.

"Just answer him," said Gary.

"Well, of course she's pretty," said Ella. "She's well-fed, isn't she? And blessed with her mother's good looks. Golden hair. Eyes like bits of winter sky in her face. She's beautiful."

"You say the governess hasn't sorted out her... little problem?" said Pete.

Ella laughed. "Not yet, but she will," she said, her voice laced with bitterness. "That friend of hers turned out to be charitable. She'll be taken in soon. I'll only get this opportunity another two or three times, then Sally will be replaced. But I'll find the new governess's weakness. I'll get something out of it one way or another."

"Then we've got to move quickly," said Gary.

"Move quickly? What are you talking about?" asked Ella.

Fred folded his arms. "How would you like to make some extra money, Ella?"

"I told you, I already am," said Ella proudly, lifting her bottle to her lips. "I don't need your help."

Fred raised an eyebrow. "Not even if I was to give you fifty pounds?"

"Fifty pounds!" Ella spat beer all over the table. "Where would you get fifty pounds?"

"That would just be your cut," said Fred, his eyes gleaming.

Ella put the bottle down. "I'm listening."

"A housekeeper approached us last week when we were mending a fence for one of the fancy houses on the other end of London," said Gary. "A pretty, prim lady – not the type to talk to us. But she was desperate, she said."

"Her master and mistress had just suffered an awful tragedy," said Pete. "They'd tried for years to have a child, and with great difficulty, they'd finally had one. A little girl. The doctors said that the mistress could never have a baby again without terrible threat to her life, but they were happy. At least they had their little girl."

"Until they didn't," said Fred. "See, just a couple of weeks ago, the little one died. Consumption. Nothing that could be done. They're utterly devastated. The mistress won't get out of bed; the master has locked himself in his study."

"So, what does that have to do with anything?" asked Ella.

"The housekeeper came to us with a simple request," said Pete. "She just wants a child for her master and mistress to adopt. A little girl – pretty, like the last one. They're too broken-hearted to go to an orphanage and do it. She said she'd pay us handsomely to find a sweet orphan that needs a home."

"Trouble is, no fancy couple is going to adopt a real orphan," said Gary derisively. "They want something plump and pretty. Something like your little Lena."

Ella shook her head, remembering blood on the sheets, the midwife's haggard face. A baby that never cried. "No, no," she said. "You can't be serious. I can't steal that little thing away from her parents."

"Oh, rubbish," said Pete. "Come on, Ella."

"No, Pete," said Ella, pushing back her chair. "That's too much. I'm not above doing what I have to do to survive. Poor folk need to make a way for themselves, you know. But I know what it's like to lose a child. I'm not going to do it."

"Lose a child? Really, Ella," said Gary. "Do you think that the mistress feels the same way about her daughter as you did about your baby? She's hardly ever home, I'll bet. Them rich folks only have children to give them to governesses and forget about them."

Ella paused. "Well... that's true," she said slowly.

"And what life would that child have there, anyway?" asked Fred. "You've said it yourself − that master and mistress of yours are heartless. They pay you a pittance. You deserve better, and so does that girl. Let her go to a family that really needs her."

"I don't know..." Ella paused.

"Fifty pounds, Ella," said Gary. "Think what you could do with that money."

Ella *was* thinking. She could get away from London, away from all its dark memories, once and for all. She could go wherever she wanted. She could become whatever she wanted.

"You say they'd take good care of her?" she said doubtfully.

"Of course, they would," said Fred. "Better than if she was their own daughter."

"Come on, Ella," said Pete. "That lady is going to die of a broken heart. You could give her the will to live."

"And get fifty pounds out of it," Gary reminded her.

Ella nodded slowly. "You're right," she said. "My mistress has it coming to her, the fancy hag." She squared her shoulders. "When?"

"We'll be in touch. But it has to be before Christmas," said Pete.

"Yes," said Fred. "Let's give that sweet couple a Christmas to remember."

There was something less than charitable in the way all three of them began to chuckle. But Ella joined in, her veins coursing with excitement. Fifty pounds! It could change her life.

It would change many lives.

WHEN LENA WOKE UP, SHE THOUGHT AT FIRST THAT SHE might be alone. Sitting up in her cot, she pushed her blanket aside. "Sally?" she cried, a pang of fear running through her.

"Not here," grunted a voice from the fireplace.

Lena relaxed. "Oh, hello, Ella," she said. "Are you going to take care of me for the afternoon again?"

"Yes," said Ella. She sat up, opened her eyes, and gave Lena a long look. "And you're not going to give me any trouble, got it?"

"No, I won't," said Lena meekly. She knew that Ella wouldn't make her get up and do anything, so she lay back again, pulling up her blankets. "Where is Sally this time?"

"She's gone to walk her sister's dog," said Ella.

Lena grinned. "I love dogs," she said. "I asked Mama so nicely to bring me a puppy back from India. She said maybe she would get me a little puppy for Christmas. A soft one, small enough that I could pick him up and hug him." Not having a puppy, she hugged Mr. Mousie instead. "Don't you think that would be lovely? Can we go and see Sally's sister's dog?"

"No," said Ella.

Lena sighed. Ella was such a bore sometimes, but Sally had told her to be a good girl, so she decided not to complain.

"I can't wait for Mama and Papa to get back for Christmas," she said. "We're going to decorate all the halls, Mama said. We're going to put up holly and branches and cover the tree with candles. It's going to be so much fun." She giggled. "And I'm going to get lots and lots of presents, I just know it."

"Good for you," grunted Ella.

"I want a puppy more than anything else in the world," said Lena. "I told Mama that she doesn't have to get me anything else, not even the pink ribbons that I like or sugar sweets or even chocolates. I just want a sweet little puppy." She sat up, looking over at Ella. "What do you want for Christmas, Ella?"

Ella looked up. "What, me?"

"Yes, you." Lena smiled. "What is your mama and papa going to give you?"

Ella looked away, and Lena saw a muscle move in her cheek as she clenched her jaw. "Come on," she said, getting up. "Put on your shoes. We're going for a little walk."

"A walk?" Lena glanced out of the window. Twilight was falling, and she could see snowflakes swirling in the breeze outside. "Isn't it too cold outside?"

"No, not a bit." Ella gave her a wide, brittle smile. "It's going to be an adventure."

"Like Little Bird's adventure?" asked Lena, touching the book where it lay on her nightstand.

"Sure, if that's what you want," said Ella. "Come on."

Ella wasn't very good at putting shoes on. It took her three tries to get Lena's shoes properly over her feet, and even then, Ella's fingers seemed too big and clumsy to tie the laces neatly. Once they were finally on, Ella lifted her down from the cot.

"There," she said, running a rough hand over the top of Lena's head to smooth down her hair. "That's all right. Here's your coat. Let's go."

Ella led Lena down the big stairs and off into a hallway where Lena had never been before. She clung to Ella's hand, excited for the adventure, looking around as the hallway grew narrower. "Where are we going?" she asked.

"Through the kitchen," said Ella.

"Oh! I've never been in the kitchen," said Lena. "Is it nice?"

"I suppose," said Ella.

They stepped into a big, warm room that seemed to be so full of things Lena could hardly take them all in – stoves and fire-places and pots and pans and ham hanging from the rafters and a string of onions by the window. She wanted to look around, but Ella tugged her out into a little courtyard where there was nothing but bins, and then they were out in the street.

"I've never walked on the street before," said Lena, excited. "We've driven in the carriage, but I've never walked."

"You'll like it," said Ella. "It'll keep you warm."

"Are we going on a long walk?" asked Lena.

"No, not long. Just down to Old Nichol," said Ella. "Come on. Keep up."

"Where's that?"

"You ask too many questions." Ella sighed. "Just keep quiet."

Lena shut her mouth, but at least she could still look around. She gazed at the houses around her; some of them were nearly as grand as her own, and perhaps almost as pretty, but not quite. No house was as pretty as hers. She looked back as they turned the corner, glimpsing the towering sandstone walls and the long expanse of snow-covered lawn, hidden behind the palisades. The last thing she saw were the gateposts − each mounted by a horse's head, the stone mane tossing, the stone eyes wide − before they headed down a street she hadn't seen before.

"Oh," said Lena, as they moved out of the street and into a square. "Is this Fairyland?"

Ella laughed. "No, it isn't. It's just the marketplace."

To Lena, it looked like Fairyland. The roofs of the little buildings were covered in snow; lights and candles adorned the whole square, and there was a gigantic Christmas tree right in the middle. Horses clip-clopped merrily to and fro, blowing enchanting clouds of curling steam into the cold night air.

And there was a different smell from every shopfront – cinnamon and nutmeg, baking bread and sweet cake, holly and pine. It was all much too exciting for words.

"Can we go into the sweet shop, Ella?" Lena begged. "Oh, please, please can we?"

"Not now," said Ella. "Maybe on the way back."

Leaving the square behind, they took a sharp turn into a narrow street. There were broken boxes and old barrels lying here, and it was very, very dark. Lena hesitated, clinging tightly to Ella's hand. Ella gave her arm an impatient little yank, tugging her forward. Then, they stepped out into another street, and Lena felt as though she was looking into a different world. Everything in front of her was a mess; a great, sprawling, dirty, broken mess. She couldn't see one single thing that was whole or clean or beautiful. There was nothing but brokenness and filth: in the potholes of the streets that were filled with grayish slush, in the sagging houses that leaned on one another like a group of wounded soldiers; in the eyes and bones of the children huddling in the doorways, staring at Lena with empty eyes. They frightened her. She stopped.

"Ella, where are we?"

"Nearly there," said Ella.

"Nearly where?" Lena yanked her hand out of Ella's. "I want to go home. I'm scared."

"Don't make a fuss, Lena." Ella's eyes darted back and forth. She seized Lena's arm. "Come on."

"I don't like it here. I want to go back home," said Lena. "I want to go home to Mama and Papa and Sally."

Ella yanked her on her arm. "Shut up," she said roughly.

Suddenly, even though there were eyes staring at her from every corner, Lena felt horribly alone. She pulled back, her voice rising to a scream. "Let me go!"

"Lena!" Ella snapped.

Lena twisted, wrenching her little arm free. It slid through Ella's rough fingers, and she bolted back toward that pretty marketplace, her feet squelching in the slush. She had just glimpsed the warm light from the marketplace when two iron hands closed over both her arms and she was lifted into the air, spun around, and slammed against the nearest wall.

"Hush!" roared an angry voice, a nasty, fruity smell washing over Lena. She froze, petrified, staring at the man who had pinned her down. He was skinny, with long yellow teeth like a horse.

"Don't hurt her, Fred!" said Ella, breathlessly.

"I thought you said she wasn't going to give us any trouble," Fred snapped.

"She's just scared. She's never been in this part of town," said Ella.

"Who are you?" Lena whimpered.

The man drew back his hand and slapped her. Lena had never been slapped before, and it felt horrible – stinging and painful and terrible. She froze, speechless.

"Don't hurt her, Fred!" Ella shouted. "Come on. Give her back to me. I'll take her home."

Fred sneered. "It's too late for that now, sis. You can't get cold feet now."

"I didn't think you would hurt her. I don't care about the money anymore," said Ella. "Just give her to me."

Fred laughed, but there was nothing warm or playful about it. It sounded more like an old dog barking. He reached into his pocket and pulled out a little bag that jingled, tossing it at Ella.

"There you are," he said. "That's what you wanted, isn't it?"

Ella picked it up and hurled it back at his head. "Give me back the girl!"

"Too late now," said Fred. He put Lena down, keeping an iron grip on her arm. "Take your money and go."

"Please, Fred," Ella begged. "Please, give her to me. I-I made a mistake."

Fred ignored her. Turning, he moved away. Lena screamed as he yanked on her arm.

"Ella!" she shrieked. "Ella!"

"Lena!" Ella lunged forward. "Let her go, you monster!" She clawed at Fred's arm, and he spun around. His fist met her cheekbone with a meaty thump, and Ella fell to the floor. She didn't move.

"Ella!" Lena shrieked.

"Shut up!" Fred shook her, making her teeth rattle. "Do you want another slap?"

Lena fell silent, her heart pounding. Ella was groaning, but she didn't move. Fred laughed, bent down and grabbed the bag of money, tucking it back into his pocket.

"Stupid," he muttered, then spat on the ground by Ella's head. "Come on," he added, moving off into the darkness. "You're coming with me."

And there was nothing, nothing at all, that Lena could do about it.

CHAPTER 6

Lena didn't think her legs could carry her much further. She kept trying to make them move, keeping her feet underneath her, because ever since hitting Ella, Fred had not slowed down. Lena had the feeling that if she didn't stay upright, he'd simply drag her.

The icy wind was starting to work its way underneath her coat now, poking its cold fingers inside to stroke her back and belly with a frigid touch. She looked up at the tall man beside her, feeling his fingers closed like a shackle around her arm.

"I'm cold," she whispered.

Fred made no reply. Instead, he just turned down yet another grisly little side street. They had been marching through this terrifying place for what felt like hours, but there seemed to be fresh horrors around every corner, at every turn. The stench was worse than anything Lena had ever smelled before; she didn't know where it was coming from, but it filled the air, seeming to pervade every surface.

The houses all had broken windows that stared down at her like eye sockets. They were scary, but the men and women that huddled on the street, perched on little piles of rags and trying to warm their hands at tiny fires that sputtered in the snow, were far worse. There was a hunger in them that made Lena feel like they might jump up and claw at her at any moment.

"Why are the people outside?" she asked. "It's so cold. Why don't they go into their houses?"

"They don't have houses," said Fred impatiently.

Lena didn't understand. "But why don't they have houses? They need them."

Fred didn't answer. Lena wanted to ask more, but she was too tired now, and hunger was clawing at her stomach. They rounded a little bend in the street – if you could call it that; it was little more than a muddy footpath, pockmarked by puddles of slush and nameless ooze – until they reached a dead end. At the very end of the path stood a rickety house. It was taller than the other buildings, perhaps three stories, but Lena could see that its front door was tied with a bit of string.

Fred knocked on the door. Splinters flaked off it, drifting down onto the grubby threshold.

"It's me," he shouted. "I've got a delivery for you."

Lena pulled back. Was she the delivery? Ominous footsteps sounded on the corridor, and she felt her heart hammering in her chest. What was about to come to that door? Was it the big bad wolf?

"I want to go home," she whimpered.

The door opened, and Lena cringed. But the face that peered at her from over a pair of half-moon spectacles was kindly, framed by a bush of silver curls. Plump, red cheeks crinkled as the old lady smiled.

"Oh, she's just perfect!" she said.

Lena felt herself relax just a little. Fred pushed her forward. "There you go," he said. "Now, the other half."

The old lady gave a gentle titter. "Business is business." She handed Fred a pouch of coins. "And mind you keep your mouth shut, dear."

Fred grinned. The expression reminded Lena of the big bad wolf's snarl in the book about the little bird. "Silence is good for business. Let me know when I can bring you another."

The old lady reached out, grabbing Lena's arm. She'd expected a warm touch like Mama's, but instead the old lady's hand felt like talons. "She'd better last longer than the previous one, you hear?"

"She will. She's been well looked after." Fred laughed. Then he turned away and trudged off, tucking the pouch into his jacket and whistling cheerfully.

Lena looked up at the old lady. "Who are you?" she asked softly.

"Delilah Darling, my dear. But you can call me Auntie D." The old lady smiled. "Come in out of the cold, now."

Lena allowed herself to be led into the corridor. The single gas lamp on the wall bathed them in an inadequate, weak light that only seemed to highlight the cracks in the walls. Floorboards squealed in pain underneath Auntie D's feet as she marched off, Lena following closely in her wake.

"I'm lost," Lena told her, clinging to her skirts. "I want to go home to my mama and papa's house. I'm not supposed to be here."

Auntie D stepped into another room. It was very dark. "Don't you worry, dear," she said. "We'll take care of you."

"I'm hungry," Lena whispered.

"I'm sure you are." Auntie D gave a laugh, and something about it was different. It didn't sound like she found anything funny. "Hunger is good for you."

A match flared in the darkness, and Auntie D lit a candle, lifting it up onto a dresser nearby. Lena couldn't believe her eyes. The room they were in was small – perhaps half the size of the nursery – but it contained more children than she'd ever seen at once before. She tried to count, but it made her head spin, because they were all so... so dirty. So pale. They looked like the children she'd seen on the streets making her way here.

"Is this the new one?"

The harsh, masculine voice came from the doorway. Lena whipped around, petrified. The man in the doorway was also elderly, his thin strands of white hair combed over a shiny, bald crown. He had long, gnarled fingers and ice-blue eyes that burned with cold.

"This is her. Looks good, don't she?" asked Auntie D.

"Who are you?" Lena gasped.

The man ignored her. "A little too good, if you ask me," he said. "People will be suspicious."

"You're right." Auntie D turned to her, giving her a long look. "We'd best fix that." Then she reached out, grasped one of the pink ribbons in Lena's left pigtail, and yanked.

"Ouch!" Lena yelped, hearing her own hair ripping. "You're hurting me!"

Auntie D tossed the pretty ribbon on the floor and dug her pudgy fingers into Lena's neatly combed hair. Lena squealed and pulled back, but the man's bony hand shot out, seizing her by the arms. It was no use struggling. Auntie D ripped at Lena's hair, yanking strands loose to hang around her face.

Her hair ruined, Lena struggled harder, but the more she screamed, the tighter the old man gripped her arms. Next, Auntie D seized Lena's right sleeve and pulled. A long rip appeared in the shoulder of her dress.

"There," said Auntie D, stepping back and staring down at Lena. "Much better."

Lena was shaking. Her scalp and arms ached. "I want my mama," she whispered.

The old man laughed. He let her go, shoving her deeper into the room. "You're never going to see your mama again," he said. "And it's no use crying about it." Then he slammed the door behind him so hard that the candle flame flickered.

Tears poured down Lena's cheeks. She couldn't understand why Auntie D and that awful man had pulled at her hair and ripped her dress. Sally would be so upset when she saw the torn dress. She reached for the doorknob; it was just out of reach, but she managed to grab it on the second try and pulled. The door didn't budge.

"It's locked," snapped a voice from inside the room. "Stop trying."

Lena turned. The girl who spoke was a little older than she was. She sat on a hard sleeping pallet, a single blanket tucked around her shoulders.

"We're tired," she said. "Go to sleep."

"I don't want to go to sleep," Lena whispered. "I want to go home."

"You're not going home. Just be quiet. We're tired," the girl repeated.

Lena was tired, too. She wanted so much to climb into her nice, warm bed, but right now even these sleeping pallets looked inviting as her little legs ached from the long walk. Yet every pallet seemed to have a child already sitting on it. Lena would have loved to cuddle up to the girl who'd spoken, but her eyes were as hard as flint. As cold as iron. Looking from one child to the other, Lena saw that all of them looked that way – angry and frightening. And desperate.

All of them but for one. A boy, sitting on a pallet right at the very back of the room. Lena couldn't tell if his eyes were hard, because they were closed; his knees were drawn up to his chest, his forehead resting on them. Not knowing what else to do, Lena picked her way between the pallets to him.

"Excuse me?" she whispered.

The boy looked up. He didn't say anything, but he had soft gray eyes that reminded her of Mr. Mousie and a scar underneath his cheek. The scar looked sad and painful, but his eyes won her over.

"Please may I lie down here?" Lena whispered.

The boy still didn't speak. He just moved over, patting the blanket beside him. Lena climbed onto the pallet and curled up; she could feel the wooden slats poking into her side, but it was a relief simply not to be on her feet.

"I'm Lena," she murmured. "What's your name?"

The boy gave a tiny sigh. He was a little older than her, just old enough that where his hand rested on her shoulder, it felt big and reassuring.

"Farley," he said.

Lena had so many more questions. Why was she here? Who were those people? When could she go home to her mama? But she was much too tired to ask. Sleep came straight for her, and its darkness was mercy.

❧

LENA HAD NEVER BEEN SO COLD. SHE SHIVERED, HER ARMS wrapped around herself, staring out at the street in front of her. It seemed like a different world from the one through which Auntie D and the man – whom Lena had been told was called Judas – had led her from the tenement a few minutes ago. Here, there were cobblestones, and Christmas lights, and ladies in pretty dresses like Mama's, walking from one shopfront to the next.

She wanted to run up to the nearest lady, to tell her everything. To beg for help. But the savage look in Judas's eyes stopped her as he crouched down to her level, an ominous shadow in the dark alley where she was hiding along with the couple and six of the other children.

"Now, Lena, do you remember what to do?" Judas asked.

Lena didn't want to remember – or to do anything that Judas was telling her to do. But her leg still stung from the pinch Auntie D had given her when she'd tried to refuse, so she tucked her small hands under her cheek and tilted her head to one side.

"Alms?" she whispered. "Alms for a hungry child?"

Judas looked up at Auntie D, and they exchanged a grin. "She's got potential, this one." He nodded at her. "Exactly like that. And then what do you do?"

"I put the money in here." Lena picked up the holey tin cup at her feet.

"Good." Judas nodded. "Now go out onto the corner that I showed you, and you do exactly as you're told."

Lena nodded eagerly. She would run out onto that corner. She would be ready to grab the nearest kind-looking lady's hand and beg to be taken home.

"And don't get any ideas of running away," said Judas. He reached down, grabbing the front of Lena's dress, his grip so tight that it made it hard to breathe. She stared into his eyes, terrified. Had he read her mind? "I promise you, there's no way you can run faster than me," he snarled in her face, a foul stench of tobacco huffing into her face on his warm breath. "I will catch you, and I will punish you."

The look in his blue eyes froze Lena to the very bone. She knew, in that moment, that he would make good on that promise. No matter how much space she had around her, Lena was undeniably trapped.

"Now go." Judas let her go, giving a sharp laugh. "Go and make money."

He gave her a push between the shoulder blades, and Lena staggered out onto the street. Her legs were stiff from the day before, and she tottered toward the corner by the bakery Judas had shown her. The delicious scent of fresh bread filled the air, reminding her of how hungry she was. But she knew she couldn't go inside. All she could do was to stand where Judas had told her and hold up her tin cup, searching the faces of the crowd bustling by.

"Alms? Alms for a hungry child?" she moaned, her tone laced with hunger. She didn't know what alms were, but she hoped that she could eat them. She had never been so hungry in her life. "Alms?"

A lady stopped, tugging at her husband's arm. "Oh, George!" she cried. "Just look at the poor little thing."

"Ignore her, Mabel," said the husband roughly. "Beggars are ruining this city. The government should do something about them."

"But look at her," said Mabel. "She's so hungry." She came over to Lena, opening her purse. "You're such a sweet thing," she sighed, dropping a few coins into Lena's cup.

"Th-thank you, ma'am," said Lena.

"And such beautiful manners." Mabel's brow furrowed. "How did you end up here, honey?"

Lena's heart thumped. She looked over at the alleyway, knowing Judas was glaring at her. What should she do?

"Mabel, come." George tugged at the nice lady's arm. "Let's go."

Lena watched them go, her heart feeling like it might just tumble out of her chest and shatter on the ground like a dropped snow globe. She swallowed hard, holding up the cup again, terrified that Judas would find and punish her.

"Alms?" she tried again. "Alms?" If she shook the cup, it made a little rattling noise. "Alms for a hungry child?"

That morning was the longest of Lena's entire life. Hour after hour dragged by. Her toes first burned with the cold, then ached, and then went entirely numb. Her knees cramped from standing in the cold, but every time she looked back toward the alleyway, Judas or Auntie D was there to glare at her, freezing her in place with fear. The cup got heavier as one lady after another dropped coins into it, and soon even a few of the men had given her something. One gave her a piece of bread. She ate it before even thinking about it, but at least Judas didn't come out and beat her for it.

Her voice was getting hoarse as she spotted a gentleman hurrying along the street, looking at his pocket-watch. She stepped out in front of him, shaking the cup. "Alms?" she tried.

The gentleman looked up, and his lip curled in an angry sneer. "Get away!" he ordered.

"Oh, please, sir," Lena whispered, her eyes filling with tears. "Please?" She held up the cup.

The gentleman grabbed her shoulder and shoved. "Get away!" he shouted.

Lena fell heavily on her hands and knees. Her knees were so cold that the impact brought with it a pain that took her breath away. Still clutching the cup, she sat up, seeing blood spread through her stockings. Tears coursed down her cheeks. Breathless with pain, sobbing, she ran back toward the alleyway.

"Auntie D! Judas!" she whimpered, holding out her arms to be picked up.

She wasn't. Instead, the back of Judas's hand lashed across her face, knocking her over backward. For the second time, Lena slammed into the ground. The cup tumbled out of her fingers and coins sprayed across the dirt.

"You stupid child!" Judas spat. "What are you thinking?"

"You will never run toward us!" shouted Auntie D. "You will stay where you're put and do exactly as you're told – or we'll make you pay for it." Her eyes were icy behind her spectacles. She pulled up her sleeves and grabbed her walking stick. "Just like you'll pay for it now."

Lena cried out, cowering against the ground as Auntie D came nearer, her walking stick raised. Lena had nowhere to run. Her knees burned and there was blood in her mouth, but she knew that was nothing compared to what was coming—

"Look!"

It was the second word that Lena had ever heard Farley speak. He was breathless, on his hands and knees on the alley, sweeping the coins that had spilled out of the cup into a pile.

"Look at this!" he said. "Look how much she's earned!" He looked up, and his gray eyes were alight with desperation.

Auntie D lowered her walking stick. "Well," she said, surprised. "Look at that!"

Judas strode over to Farley, shoving him carelessly out of the way. He laughed, scooping up a fistful of coins. "Almost more than the cup could hold!" He grinned at Auntie D. "We've stumbled upon a goldmine, Delilah."

Farley scrambled to his feet and came over to where Lena still lay, sobbing. He knelt beside her, lifted her to her feet, wrapped his arms around her. "It's all right, Lena," he whispered. "It's all right."

Lena threw her arms around his neck and buried her face in his chest. It had never felt further from all right.

"LENA!" CHARLES SHOUTED, PEERING INTO THE BUSHES. "Lena!"

He could hear his wife, Joan, calling over on the other end of the park. Her thin voice was hoarse with crying and hollering, but there was still such a deep love in her tremulous tone as she cried their daughter's name over and over among the trees. Charles used his cane to push aside some of the bushes.

What a welcome home from India this was. It was a nightmare—a raging nightmare. His precious girl been gone for more than twenty-four hours by then. *More than twenty-four hours.* Snow dusted down on his shoes as he searched among the leaves, praying with all his heart that a pair of sky-blue eyes would look up at him. That two little arms would be stretched out toward him, a piping voice saying, *You found me, Papa!* as if this were nothing more than a game of hide and seek.

But there was nothing in the bushes, nothing but an old bone and a scrap of discarded cloth. Charles backed away, swamped by a feeling of overwhelming weariness.

"Oh, Lena," he whispered, gazing out across the snowy park. His and Joan's footprints crisscrossed every part of it. "Where are you?"

His heart was like a cannonball in his chest, slowing him down as he trudged back across the park to where Joan was searching underneath the pine trees. She peered up into the branches, as if a five-year-old girl could have climbed so high.

"Lena!" she shouted, her voice full of fear.

"Joan, darling." Charles could barely summon the energy to speak. He reached out, touching her arm. "She's not here."

Joan turned. Fresh tears were glittering on her cheeks. "Oh, Charles, then where is she?" she pleaded. "We can't give up. No one has found a trace of her, but she *has* to be here. She has to be *somewhere*."

"I don't know, my love." Charles swallowed hard. "But we'll find her. We will." He wrapped an arm around her shoulders, leading her back toward the street.

Joan's shoulder shook with the force of the sobs she was holding back. She squared them, wiping at her tears. "Where shall we try next?" she asked.

Charles gazed at her admiringly. Her amber eyes were fierce, her blonde hair the same shade of perfect gold as Lena's. He had never known the strength that was deep within his wife until that moment. Kissing the side of her head, he pulled her closer. "Let's think logically," he said. "We've questioned all of the staff. They all saw her and Sally playing on the lawn that morning, but not after nap time."

"Where would Sally have taken her?" asked Joan. "Perhaps to the shops?"

"Maybe, although I can't think why." Charles sighed. "It's worth a try, though."

"Anything is worth a try to find our little girl." Joan bit her lip. "Oh, Charles, what more can we do? We've already spoken to the police. They're already searching for her – and for Sally. Even Sally's parents haven't seen her. Where is my girl, Charles? *Where?*"

"Please, don't worry." Charles squeezed her shoulders. "I'll pour every cent of my fortune into this if I have to. We're going to get her back."

"But what if..." Joan stopped.

"Don't," said Charles. He'd thought of all those what-ifs already: what if they had been run over, what if they had been robbed, what if his beautiful, sweet, loving little girl was lying at the bottom of the ugly Thames? "Don't do it to yourself, Joanie," he said firmly. "We're going to find her."

"We *have* to find her," Joan choked out. Her tears overwhelmed her, her body shaking with the force of her grief. "Oh, why did we ever go to India? Why did I ever let my little girl out of my sight?"

Charles's own heart felt ripped, brutally torn into a thousand bleeding pieces. "I would give anything to have her in my arms again," he said.

"I would give anything," Joan agreed. "And I would never, ever let her go."

CHAPTER 7

Lena gazed down into the small wooden bowl that she clutched in both of her hands. It had only gotten colder and darker in the tenement. She wasn't sure how much time had passed since she'd first been brought there, but she knew that there were more and more Christmas decorations out on the streets, and that Judas and Auntie D were cooking something that smelled delicious. Roast goose, maybe. Or perhaps even pork.

Her stomach growled at the wonderful smell, but she knew it wasn't for her or for any of the other children standing in line for their dinner. The other pot was for them, the one that bubbled ominously. Lena didn't even care how tasteless her dinner would be. She just hoped that perhaps, just today, Auntie D would be a little bit generous with the helpings. Although maybe even that wouldn't help. Lena felt she could eat six bowls of gruel and still the great pit in her stomach wouldn't be filled.

"I'm so hungry," she whispered, under her breath so that Auntie D and Judas didn't hear. She'd learned the hard way that complaining was likely to earn her a box on the ear.

Her words were meant for Farley's ears. He stood right behind her, close enough that his bowl gently bumped her back when he moved. "Almost time for supper," he whispered back.

"Why do we only get to eat gruel, Farley?" Lena twisted to look up at him. "Why don't we get to have delicious food like them?"

"They're selfish, Lena," said Farley quietly. "They want to keep the best food for themselves."

"Then why do we get so little?"

Farley sighed. "They want us to be skinny and hungry. Then people give us more money."

Lena couldn't understand. Why did they need to get even more money if Auntie D and Judas already had everything they needed? She was grateful for Farley explaining things to her, though. Asking questions was a sure way to get a cuff or a slap from Judas.

"How come you know so much about them?" she asked.

"I've been here a long time," said Farley. He smiled. "That's why it's nice to have a friend."

Farley's eyes were sad, but his smile made Lena feel a little better. "Friends are good," she said. "I have lots of friends back home. Maybe you can meet them when my mama and papa find me."

"You have a mama and papa?" asked Farley.

"Don't you?"

"Well..." Farley stopped. "I suppose I must, but I don't remember them."

"You can share my mama and papa with me, then," said Lena gently. "They'll be looking for me. I wasn't supposed to go with Ella, but I did. But they'll be back from India, because it's nearly Christmas, and they'll find us."

"Of course, they will," said Farley, smiling. "And then they'll take you home and you can have all the roast goose and stuffing that you want."

Lena reached for Farley's hand, gripping it tightly. "And you'll be there, too," she said quietly. "We'll all be there, and it'll be safe and warm, and we'll have enough to eat."

She didn't really believe her own words until she saw the light behind Farley's smile. "Of course," he said. "Of course, we will."

ELLA TRIED NOT TO LISTEN TO THE QUIET SOBBING COMING

from the settee by the fire. She focused her attention on dusting the Nativity scene that had been set up by the Christmas tree, gently flicking away dust from the donkey's ears as it gazed in delighted adoration at the little porcelain crib containing a haloed Babe.

She raised a hand to the aching welt on her cheekbone. It hurt, but not as much as her heart. Yet this was not just about the money – when she woke up in the alleyway, it was all gone, and so was Fred and Lena. This was a raw, familiar ache, something she'd known so well when she'd clutched her still-born child to her chest and screamed her agony out to the world. She'd tried so hard to keep it all buried, to keep the world at arm's length so that it could never hurt her again. Yet somehow that little girl with the golden hair had crawled deep underneath Ella's best defences.

Another of the parlour-maids came in. Her face was haggard, and Ella saw the deepest pity in her eyes as she gazed at the mistress who sat crying on the settee. She was carrying a silver tray, and she set it gently down on the table by the settee.

"Here, ma'am," she said softly. "Your supper."

Joan paused in her crying just long enough to lower her hands from her face. Ella had never seen her look anything but composed, but now her face was mottled and blotchy, her eyes raw.

"Oh, no thank you," she said faintly. "I'm not hungry."

The maid hesitated, knowing she was overstepping her bounds. "Ma'am, please," she said softly. "You didn't have anything at lunch either."

"She's right, my love." Charles got up from the armchair, where he'd been frantically scouring the newspaper. He sat down beside Joan, putting an arm around her shoulders. "You'll make yourself ill. You need your strength."

"I know, I know." Joan groaned, hiding her face back in her hands. "But I just can't face it, Charles. I... I have no appetite. I just want Lena back."

Ella felt tears choking at her throat as she turned back to the Nativity scene. She dusted the face of the Baby, and even those porcelain eyes seemed to be staring into her very soul. She'd tried so hard to forget about it all, knowing her brothers would be angry if she confronted them about the money. *That nice couple is overjoyed this Christmas because they have a child again,* she tried to remind herself. *You've done good.* But Joan's quiet crying in the background made the attempt seem shallow and flat.

There was a quiet knock on the doorframe. The butler, Godfrey, was standing there, his face pale and pained. "Sir," he said.

"What is it?" asked Charles.

"It's..." Godfrey paused. "It's the police."

Every vestige of colour drained from Charles's face. "Show them in," he said, his voice strangled.

Ella paused, waiting, her body suddenly pulled as tight as a cello string. She had a terrible, terrible feeling in her stomach, one that she could see mirrored in Joan's frightened eyes as she rose to her feet. She and Charles faced the door together, like two convicted prisoners facing the gallows.

The policeman stepped inside, his uniform dusted with snow, and Ella could read the answer in his eyes even before he spoke.

"Sergeant," said Charles, his voice still strained. "What is it?"

"Mr. Phillips, I'm so terribly sorry." The sergeant took off his hat and tucked it under his arm. "We... we've found a body in the river." He swallowed visibly. "A little girl."

Neither of them screamed. It would have been easier somehow if only they had screamed, but they didn't. Joan did not make a sound. She simply crumpled, like a lily in a strong wind, her strong and elegant posture crushed in an instant to the floor. Charles barely seemed to notice his wife collapsing beside him. His face went grey, and he said nothing. Turning on his heel, he strode out of the parlour and into the adjoining study. He did not slam the door, but the quiet thud it made when it closed reverberated through the entire house.

Ella didn't realize that she'd dropped the duster in her hands until it fell softly to the floor. She stared down at it, her heart hammering the same staccato beat over and over in her chest. *I did this. I did this. I did this.* She had killed that sweet, beautiful little girl as surely as if her own hands had flung her into that river. The sergeant was still in the room, kneeling with Godfrey and the maid by Joan's fallen figure. She should go up to him. Tell him what she'd done. Tell him it was her fault. Face the justice for what she'd done.

But somehow, her feet just wouldn't move her forward. She couldn't face the fact that she had done to another mother the thing that had shattered her entire being. So she just turned and ran – out of the parlour, down the long corridor, through the big main doors, across the snowy lawn, into the street. Away from everything she had done.

And she was never coming back.

PART II

CHAPTER 8

Seven Years Later

"WHAT SHALL WE SING NEXT?" LENA ASKED, TRYING TO sound more enthusiastic than she felt.

There was no response from the row of hollow-eyed children sitting in front of her. They wrapped their arms around their skinny bodies, unimpressed by Lena's and Farley's efforts. Looking into their eyes, Lena had that same feeling she always had when she was trying to help the other children who'd been trapped along with her and Farley in the clutches of Judas and Auntie D: a feeling like she was trying to fill a gaping abyss by throwing pebbles into it, one by one.

"I don't want to sing," sighed a little boy. He was one of the younger ones – about five or six, the same age Lena had been when she'd first met the couple.

"Oh, Andrew, why not?" asked Lena, bending down to scoop him up and plant him on her own skinny hip.

"I'm tired," moaned Andrew. "And I'm hungry."

"I know you are," said Farley, patting the top of the little boy's head. "But come on, Andy. It's Christmas. We've got to celebrate just a little bit."

Lena sighed inwardly, remembering the first Christmas. She'd been hopeful then—believing that her parents were still coming to find her. Yet her hope had faded as quickly and completely as her memory of them as Christmas after Christmas went by, and she'd slowly come to learn that they were never coming for her. Her parents had given up on her, and she was stuck here for the rest of her life, begging on the streets for the couple who was feasting in the room next door.

"What about 'Hark the Herald Angels Sing'?" Lena asked. "I know most of the words from when we were begging outside the church this morning."

"That was a beautiful one," Farley agreed. "Come on, Andy. Sing with us."

He raised his gentle voice so that it rose like a thread of golden smoke through the damp and mouldy room, pressing its fingers to stop the holes in the walls and the cracked pane of the single window, seeming to soothe even the harsh lines and hard corners of the sleeping pallets where the children sat. "Hark! The herald angels sing, 'Glory to the new-born King! Peace on earth, and mercy mild, God and sinners reconciled'."

"Joyful, all ye nations, rise," Lena joined in, reaching for Farley's hand. "Join the triumph of the skies; with th' angelic host proclaim, 'Christ is born in Bethlehem'."

Mumbling and stumbling, the children tried to join in with the single stanza of the song that Lena had managed to memorize. She didn't know for sure what the angels were singing about, or who the new-born King was, but she did know there was something in the words of the carols that they heard on the street – something in the gingerbread men hanging from the Christmas trees and in the candles that stood in every window – that was bigger than her suffering.

She felt it every Christmas, and every Christmas it brought her something that was terribly scarce in the life of want and struggle she and Farley had found themselves caught up in. She wasn't sure what it was, this breath of fresh air in her soul. It was a little like wishing, although why exactly she should wish for anything at all, Lena didn't know. Wishes didn't come true. Not for her and not for any of the rest of them.

They made it through two more carols before the smaller ones started to drop off to sleep. Lena laid little Andrew on his pallet, pulling his threadbare blanket around him. He stirred in his sleep as she tucked him in, and she sighed, pushing his unkempt hair out of his pinched little face.

"I wonder where they stole you from," she murmured.

"Sometimes I wonder where they stole me from, too," said Farley softly, sitting down on his pallet opposite Lena's and Andrew's.

Lena leaned back against the wall, letting her head tip back to rest her aching neck. "Every year I can remember a little less about my home and family," she said quietly. "I remember Ella taking me away. And I... I know I had a mama. I know she used to read me a story every night about a little bird who was blown out of his nest." She smiled at the memory.

"How old are we now, do you think?" asked Farley.

"I don't know," said Lena. "I must be..." She tried to think. "Has it been six or seven Christmases?"

"I'm not sure," said Farley. "That makes you – eleven? Twelve?"

"Then you must be about thirteen," said Lena. "Maybe fourteen."

Farley sighed. "Part of me wishes I was still little. Then I could still be begging instead of stealing."

"I suppose Judas thinks little children get more money."

"They do. That's why he teaches everyone how to steal when

we outgrow begging." Farley shook his head. "I hate it, Lena. Begging was bad enough. But stealing... I don't know much, but I do know stealing is wrong. Especially when everything we steal goes to Judas and Auntie D so that they can buy more things for themselves."

"I don't want to learn to steal," said Lena quietly. "I'd hate it."

"You would, but it's better than..." Farley stopped.

Lena swallowed, remembering. It was a little more than a year ago that one of the girls had proven to be useless at stealing. Auntie D and Judas had simply left her out on the street one day, locking her out of the tenement. She'd run away at first, but then she'd come back, hungry and desperate. She had been waiting for them outside the tenement every morning for weeks, begging for scraps. Lena had tried to smuggle a few things for her, but she'd been beaten. The next morning, the girl was just a frozen body at the bottom of the steps. When they came back from begging that evening, even her body was gone.

"They won't do that to you," said Farley quickly. He reached for Lena's hand, gripping it. "They won't. I won't let it happen. If they start teaching you how to steal, I'll show you how. I'm good at it – you'll be all right."

"But you must stay good at it, Farley," said Lena, a film of tears blinding her eyes. "You mustn't grow any bigger so you can't fit down smokestacks or through windows anymore, do you hear? You need to be good, so they don't throw you out."

Farley smiled, his grey eyes dancing above the ugly scar on his cheek. "They won't throw me out," he said. "I'm much too good at stealing. Don't you worry. I'll never leave you, Lena. Never."

Lena swallowed hard. "You can't," she said. "I don't know what I'd do without you."

"Oh, Lena." Farley reached up, hooking a lock of her dirty hair behind her ear. "You'd be strong, because you are strong. I just know it. But I won't leave you. I'll always be here for you."

"Thank you, Farley," Lena whispered.

Farley lay back, pulling up his blanket. "Merry Christmas, Lena," he said quietly.

Lena lay down, curling her body around Andrew's for warmth. She pillowed her head on her arm, not having anywhere else to rest it. "Merry Christmas," she whispered.

Sleep stole quietly toward her, tugging at the edges of her consciousness. Her breathing had slowed when Farley spoke quietly again.

"What happened to the little bird?"

"What?" Lena mumbled sleepily.

"The bird in the story. You said he was blown out of his nest. So what happened to him after that?"

Lena closed her eyes, her heart hurting with the memory. "He flew back home," she whispered.

⚜

"CATCH ME IF YOU CAN, MAMA!" LENA GIGGLED, RUNNING across the soft grass, which was cool underneath her bare feet. "See if you can catch me!"

"You little rascal!" Mama was laughing. Her eyes were amber, alight with love. She ran after Lena, her arms held out. "I'm going to get you!"

Lena squealed with enjoyment. She ducked behind a pine tree, hiding with her back pressed to its rough bark, panting with effort. After a few moments, though, Mama still hadn't come for her. Lena peered around the tree. "Mama?"

"No... I'm not coming to find you." Mama's voice echoed through Lena's mind. Suddenly, the green lawn was gone. The whole world had gone dark. "I don't care. I'm not coming to find you, Lena."

"Mama!" Tears were pouring down Lena's cheeks. "No! Come back! I need you!"

"I'm not coming," said Mama. "I'm never coming for you."

"What did I do wrong? Why don't you want me?" Lena screamed. "Come back! Mama! MAMA!"

"Lena!"

Lena sat up, gasping. Farley was clutching her shoulders, his eyes worried. "Are you all right?"

"Y-yes." Lena was shaking. She could feel the sweat soaking through her dress. Wiping her brow, she glanced down at Andrew; in the scraps of moonlight, she could see that the little boy was still asleep. "I'm all right."

"You were dreaming," said Farley gently. "You were only dreaming."

Lena sat back, leaning against the wall. "I dreamed of my mama."

Farley didn't say anything. His moon-grey eyes were fixed on her, listening.

"Why didn't she come to find me, Farley?" Lena whispered. "I wish I didn't remember her at all, the way you don't remember your family. If only I didn't know that I had a mama and papa, maybe it wouldn't be so unbearable to know that they've never come for me." She swallowed. "That they didn't care enough to look for me."

"Maybe they did," said Farley gently. He took her hand. "Hold onto hope, Lena. Maybe they're still looking for you all these years later. It's a big city, and we've moved so many times over the past years as Auntie D and Judas try to keep us away from the police."

"I don't know," said Lena softly. "It's been such a long time.

They would have found me by now if they'd only looked hard enough."

"Don't cry, Lena." Farley wiped a tear from her cheek. "Remember that little bird. You'll fly home someday."

His words made her feel better, even though she didn't believe them. "Thank you, Farley," she said softly.

The scream echoed around the tenement. Gasping, children sat up all across their sleeping pallets. Lena seized Farley's hand, trembling. "What was that?"

"Stay here," Farley ordered, getting to his feet.

"No!" Lena clung to him. "I'm coming with you."

"All right, but be quiet," said Farley.

Lena held onto his hand as he made his way out of the room, heading out into the rest of the building. Her heart was hammering in her chest. The scream came again – it was hoarse and terrified, and it came from outside. "NO!" it shrieked, a youthful voice. "NO!"

Farley gasped. "Rodney."

Lena's heart sank. Farley broke into a run, and Lena held on tightly, following him down the stairs to the entrance of the tenement. The doorway was etched in moonlight, painting a scene that made Lena sick to her stomach. Rodney, one of the older boys, was being dragged outside. Judas had him by the hair and the seat of his trousers; Rodney was clinging to the doorframe, petrified of the cold night outside.

"Stop struggling!" Judas grunted.

"No! Don't throw me out! Please!" Rodney begged. "I'll freeze out there. Please!"

Judas gave another mighty tug. Rodney's fingers slipped from the frame, and he was thrown heavily onto the street on his face. As quickly as he had fallen, Rodney was scrambling to his feet, blood running from his split lip.

"No! Let me back inside!" he begged.

Judas guarded the doorway. "Get out of here!" he shouted.

"Please. I'll do anything," Rodney pleaded. "Anything you want."

"You're too old to beg, and you're no good at stealing. You're nothing to me," spat Judas. "Go!"

Rodney started forward, as if to rush into the house. Judas bent, grabbing half a brick from the floor, and hurled it at Rodney's head. It narrowly missed, clipping his shoulder instead. Rodney gave a howl of pain, grabbing at his shoulder. He hesitated, shivering in the cold winter air, his bare feet blue on the snow.

"Get!" Judas grabbed another rock. "Get away!"

"NO!" This time, the voice was Farley's, and it was a roar of defiance. He launched himself at Judas, ripping out of Lena's grip.

"Farley!" she screamed.

But it was too late. Farley's shoulder slammed into Judas's midriff, and they both crashed to the floor, Farley on top. Judas rolled over in time for Farley to deliver a hefty punch to his upper lip. Roaring with rage, blood running between his teeth, Judas lurched upright. He was bigger than the boy, much bigger, and he grabbed Farley by the neck, both hands closing around his throat. Farley kicked and struggled, but Judas lifted him easily off the floor, slamming him against the wall.

"Do you want to defy me again, boy?" Judas spat in his face. "Do you really want to do that?"

Farley made a choking noise.

"You're killing him!" Lena cried. "Let him go!"

Judas glanced around. There was no more sign of Rodney. He pressed harder on Farley's throat, his face contorted with hatred.

"You've been trouble since the beginning," he snarled.

Farley's lips were blue, his kicks growing more and more feeble.

"No!" Lena screamed, rushing forward. Judas threw an arm

back, knocking her backwards with an effortless blow. "No one will miss you," he snarled at Farley.

"Oi!" shouted a voice in the street. "It's Christmas Eve. Don't go bringing a murder to this place now!"

Judas hesitated. Glancing down the street, he saw the same thing that Lena did: a crowd had gathered around. Their eyes were doubtful, and Lena knew that Judas was thinking about the police. He stepped back, and Farley fell to the floor in a coughing, drooling, wheezing heap.

"Mind your manners," he hissed. "Or next time won't end so well for you." Delivering a last kick to Farley's stomach, he stalked back up the stairs.

"Farley." The word felt like it had been ripped from Lena. She ran to him, grabbing his arm, pulling him to his feet.

"I'm all right," Farley wheezed. "I'm all right."

Lena looked up at the angry crowd. "Come on," she said, pulling his arm over her shoulders. "Let's get away from here."

She had never been more terrified as she stumbled up the stairs, trying to support Farley's weight. All she could think about was Rodney, out there in the cold, hurt and alone.

And about how long it would be before Farley suffered exactly the same fate.

CHAPTER 9

The black bruises around Farley's windpipe had faded to yellow, but Lena could see by the way he swallowed that it was still painful. She stood very close to him, gripping his cold hand tightly in fear. She had barely left his side since that awful night, and she didn't want to do it now, but they were about to get their orders from Auntie D and Judas, and then Farley would go off into the city somewhere to do some or another crime for them, and Lena would spend the whole day worrying. Fearing that somehow, he would not come back.

The door to Judas's and Delilah's luxurious chambers opened, and the children waiting in the cold corridor simultaneously fell silent, bracing themselves. Farley's hand closed over Lena's, the reassuring pressure of his fingers on hers giving her just a moment's courage.

Judas made no attempt to greet them. He raked them with a glance, then spoke. "You three," he said, pointing at a group of the smallest children, who huddled together like birds in the rain. "Back on the street corner where you worked yesterday."

Like Lena, the children had learned it was better not to say anything. They simply kept staring up at Judas as he turned to Lena. "You," he said. "You're too old for begging."

An icy lance pierced Lena's gut. What was he going to do to her?

"You'll stay here and teach *him*," he pointed to Andrew, "how to beg the way you used to." He gave a coarse laugh. "You were a little goldmine when you were small enough. He must be the same – or you'll both pay for it."

Lena felt an overwhelming wave of relief. She looked up at Farley, and he gave her a wink. *I told you so,* she could hear him saying.

"And you." Judas raised his chin, glaring at Farley. He didn't look away, his jaw clenched. "You're going to this address. I know you can read." Judas held out a slip of paper. "Rob it."

"A house?" said Farley, surprised.

Judas's lip curled in an evil sneer. "Do as you're told, or there will be trouble," he spat.

Farley took the paper. He didn't say anything, but his eyes were on fire.

"Now go," said Judas. "Get out of my sight."

Farley turned. Lena gripped his hand convulsively for a moment, tugging him back. "Please come back," she whispered.

For the first time, he bent down, kissing the top of her head. It made her feel surrounded by a curtain of golden light, a barrier between her and the cruelties of the world. "Of course, I will," he whispered. "I'll fly home to you."

And he was gone.

FARLEY DIDN'T COME BACK.

Even after the begging children and the pickpockets had returned, even after Lena had spent hour upon hour showing Andrew how to widen his eyes and tilt his head just so, even after darkness had come stealing across the snowbound streets of London, there was still no sign of him. And with every moment that ticked by, the hole his absence was ripping in Lena's heart grew larger and larger.

She sat on his sleeping pallet by the tiny window in the top room of the tenement, listening to the frigid wind blowing with a thin wail through the cracks in the walls. Outside, the whole world was grey with swirling snow as it came down thickly, piling upon the rooftops that surrounded her. The people scurrying along the street held newspapers over their heads as they fled to safety, their scarves trailing out behind them. Farley had neither a newspaper nor a scarf, but no matter where Lena looked, she could see no sign of his fair head.

"Lena?" Andrew called. "It's time for supper."

Lena had been so absorbed in thinking of Farley that she hadn't noticed the other children filing toward the door for their meagre rations. She paused, not wanting to peel herself away from the window, but her hunger wouldn't let her stay. Getting up, her knees stiff in the cold, she took Andrew's hand and led him out of the room.

"Where's Farley?" Andrew asked, looking up at her. "Why hasn't he come back yet?"

"I don't know, Andy." Lena swallowed hard, feeling panic clawing at her like a wild animal trying to rip its way out of her gut.

The kitchen still smelled of yesterday's roast goose. Auntie D handed out wood and tin bowls, some of them with holes in the bottom that one had to stop with a finger to keep any precious drops of food from leaking out. Lena didn't even look at hers. She was scanning the room, hoping maybe Farley had appeared. But he hadn't. There was nothing except Judas, plopping one spoonful of gruel after another into the bowls the children held out to him.

"You go first, Andy," Lena whispered, putting herself last in the line. She was going to have to do something, and she didn't want the others to get into trouble.

Andrew gratefully hurried ahead. Judas spilled a little of the boy's gruel on his arm, and he scampered back to their room, sucking the drop of gruel off his grubby sleeve. Lena held her breath as she lifted her bowl and Judas scooped some gruel into it. As soon as the food was safely in her bowl, she looked up at him, meeting his ice-blue eyes.

"Where is Farley?" she asked.

Judas froze in the motion of putting the hot spoon back into the pot. His eyes narrowed. "Are you questioning me?"

Lena squared her shoulders, even though her heart was fluttering in her chest. "Yes," she said. "Where is Farley?"

Judas gave his barking laugh. "Run away, I expect," he said. "And good riddance."

"No." Lena shook her head firmly. "Farley would never run away. He wouldn't leave me." She felt tears filling her eyes. "He wouldn't. Something's happened to him. He might be hurt. Please..." She took a deep breath, trying her best to stay calm. "Please. You have to find him."

A dangerous glint came into Judas's eye. "I *have* to?" he snarled.

"Please," Lena begged. "We have to find him."

Judas's blow came out of nowhere. The back of his hand rang across Lena's face, and she staggered back, almost falling. Her grip tightened instinctively on her bowl and she struggled to stay on her feet, desperate not to drop her only meal of the day.

Judas's teeth were bared like a wild animal's. "Get out of my sight," he spat.

"Judas, please," Lena begged.

This time it was his boot. He planted it squarely in Lena's stomach, and the pain folded her in half. Her gruel splattered on the floor, splashing her face as she fell. She had just enough time to curl up around her stomach so that Judas's next kick landed on her shins instead, and then her shoulders. Tucking her arms up over her head, Lena held still, bracing herself for each blow: her arms, her head, her back. When it was done, every part of her burned.

Judas knelt down beside her, admiring his handiwork: the welts that were quickly appearing all over Lena's skin. She did her best not to cry, but tears of pain were still rolling down her cheeks as she sat up.

"Get out of my sight," he spat.

Lena ran, as much as her legs hurt, she ran. Crashing into their room, she ignored the gasps of the other children, bolting back to the pallet by the window. But this time, she knew it would be no good to stare out of that window. She just fell onto the pallet, curling herself up, and wept.

Alone.

CHAPTER 10

One Year Later

IT WAS NEARLY CHRISTMAS AGAIN, AND SNEAKING IN AND out of houses had become Lena's specialty. She wondered if Farley had been this good at creeping through the homes and businesses he'd robbed. Waiting until all the occupants were asleep. Padding across the floor on bare feet, aware of every creaking floorboard, avoiding each one. Gently turning the doorknob. Slipping across the landing and down the stairs, quick and light as a butterfly, into the large entrance hall. From there, it was just a matter of squeezing through the bay window and Lena was out in the garden, her toes freezing on the snow. She bent quickly to put on the shoes she had hidden in her hand and then hurried out, sticking to the bare paving stones so that no one would see her footprints on the snowy lawn the next morning.

The bars of the gate were just far enough apart that Lena could fit through them if she untied her hair and turned herself sideways. Out on the street now, she paused for breath. These days, her feet found pavement instead of mud when she sneaked out onto the street in front of the house where Auntie D and Judas still kept her and the other children. Her surroundings were almost picturesque; modest homes slumbering behind snowbound lawns, their roofs dusted with snow so fine that it looked like icing sugar. With their shuttered windows and Christmas candles, the houses looked like they were all made out of gingerbread and hung in neat rows on some gigantic Christmas tree.

Lena half wished they really were made out of gingerbread. Then perhaps she could have a bite. Instead, the persistent hunger still chewed on her guts as she headed down the street, her arms wrapped around herself to ward off the creeping cold.

She knew that it was her teaching of the new children that had made Auntie D and Judas rich enough to stay in houses like these instead of the filthy tenements she'd grown up in, and the knowledge made her sick to her stomach. But what could she do? Where else did she have to go? Her family had forgotten her. They'd never come for her like Farley had said they would.

And he had never come back like he'd said he would.

She waited until she was about a block from the house before she started calling. Standing at the top of a hill, she stared down at the street that lay before her, houses on each side, leading into a park right at the bottom. Maybe he was asleep on a bench there. Maybe he was still alive.

"Farley!" she called.

Her voice bounced from one house to the other, echoing around the quiet street. A dog began to bark, and Lena tried again.

"Farley!" she shouted.

Calling at intervals, she made her way down the middle of the street, feeling the snow settle on her shoulders and the loose golden torrent of her hair. "Farley!" Every house seemed to have a holly wreath on the door; where one or two oil lamps were still lit in the windows, she could see Christmas trees, decked out with ribbons. "Farley!" Each Christmas tree had a glittering golden star on the very top, and there was an atmosphere of muted excitement, of anticipated magic that might be around every corner.

"Farley!" Lena screamed. Out here on the cold street, shivering with every step, alone and with her voice echoing fruitlessly into the park's trees, she could not feel that hopefulness. She could not feel anything except fear and desperation. Christmas had always been Farley's idea; he had been the one to lead the carols and to get the other children just a little excited. It had been a tiny spot of joy in Lena's life, but his disappearance had taken it from her. Now she felt like Christmas was firmly locked behind closed doors. It was for people who had food and friends and a home, not for people like her, who had nothing.

Not even Christmas.

Lena knew that Farley wouldn't come, not tonight. He hadn't come any of the nights that she'd spent wandering the streets and crying his name until she was completely hoarse. But she had to keep trying, because she knew he hadn't run away. Unlike her family, he cared for her. He would never leave her.

She staggered forward, hope and fear, determination and desperation clashing in her heart. And she called his name until she could call no more.

WHEN FARLEY HAD FIRST COME TO THE GREAT, GREY building through which he was now walking, it had been in desperation. He had heard of the awful conditions within the workhouse, but even those seemed better than the prospect of starving to death on the cold streets. He had heard about being separated from one's family, about the awful striped cotton uniform, about the endless work and the heartless monotony of the grey days as they dragged slowly by. He had heard about the food.

He had not been told that it was less a home for the poor than it was an inescapable prison.

Trudging along in the band of men who had just come in from yet another day of pointlessly crushing rocks, Farley kept his eyes fixed on the floor. It was better than looking around at the men who walked alongside him. The hopelessness in their eyes frightened him; he had learned that some of them had been in the workhouse for years, and he could see how it had sucked the very life out of them. It was as if they had been reduced to mere puppets, barely alive, simply existing from one day to the next as they waited for the only escape they could fathom: death.

Walking into the eating hall produced a kind of weary relief in some of the men. Farley hung back, waiting as they all but collapsed onto the hard benches at the rough wooden tables that stood in neat rows down the hall. The workhouse staff started to move silently among them, carrying bowls that smelt as bland as their contents tasted. Farley took an empty spot on the end of a table on the far side of the hall, even though his stomach was growling. He knew that there were others – boys even younger than he was, old men who could barely walk, let alone work – who needed the food more than he did.

He avoided the notice of the elderly man sitting across from him. This wasn't difficult; the old man was staring down at the surface of the table, his eyes glassy, as if he were gazing into another time. Farley wondered if he had known happiness once. If he had had a family. Maybe they'd been torn away from him on his admittance to the workhouse. At least that was one mercy for Farley – when he'd come crawling in desperation to the imposing building, there had been no one left to take away from him.

Farley felt a deep pang in his heart as a hard-eyed young man dumped a bowl of boiled meat and rice in front of him. He picked up his fork and prodded the food with little interest despite the hunger in his belly. The only person he'd ever loved was far out of his reach now. He thought back to the last time he'd seen her, to the promise he'd made to those bright blue eyes as she gazed at him, full of hope and terror. He'd told Lena that he would come back to her. And now it was a year later, and after being chased across the city by police in his bid to rob the townhouse – a chase that Farley was sure Judas and Delilah had somehow orchestrated – he still hadn't fulfilled his promise.

He spooned some of the gristly meat into his mouth and started trying to chew it, shuddering at the gravely texture between his teeth. Was Lena still teaching the little children how to beg? Or had Judas and Delilah since thrown her out into the cold? Would she be safe and warm this Christmas, or were her beautiful blue eyes clouded over with death?

Farley shook his head sharply. He couldn't think that way. The hope of getting back to Lena was the only star in his sky.

"Hey, old man," a deep voice grunted. "Give me that."

Farley looked up. The old man opposite him had lost the glazed look in his eyes. Instead, there was an expression of terror in them now as he clutched his bowl, mutely resisting despite the fact that the man sitting next to him was enormous. Shoulders bulked from years of crushing rock, face weathered and hardened by suffering, the man had little black eyes that glittered with hunger and malice as they rested on the old man's half-full bowl.

"Come on," the man grunted. "Give it to me." He balled his giant hands into fists. "Don't make me ask again."

The old man gave his food a longing glance, but he knew better than to resist. His grip loosened on the bowl, and Farley saw how thin his fingers were, how the bones in his hands stood out with the skin stretched tightly over the hollows between them. Something snapped deep in Farley's soul.

"Stop," he said.

Both the old man and his assailant looked up, wide-eyed. The big man's lips curled into a dubious sneer. "Are you really going to do this, boy?" he hissed. "What do you possibly think you could achieve?"

Farley pushed his own bowl aside. "Leave him alone, Crowther. He's just as hungry as you are." He felt disdain creep into his tone as he eyed Crowther's big muscles, realizing how he'd come across enough food to fuel that kind of bulk. "Probably more."

Muscles rippled in Crowther's shoulders, but he didn't rise. He just shook his head. "As if you could stop me," he muttered, reached over, and seized the old man's bowl.

Fire coursed through Farley's veins, spurring him to action. He lunged across the table, sending his own bowl flying, the tasteless stew splattering across the table surface. His hands closed on Crowther's wrist, his fingers barely making it all the way around.

"I told you to leave him alone!" he roared.

The big man barely twitched. It was as if Farley was just an annoying fly. His free arm swiped across, not even punching him, just bringing the back of his shovel-sized hand across Farley's face. The force of the blow threw him backwards. He felt the bench disappear from under him and land heavily on the floor, knowing a moment of fear as his back hit the ground, and then nothing but impact and pain when the back of his head cracked against the unmerciful stone.

There was yelling all around him as a legion of angry paupers rose to their feet, all of them shouting. The cries of the house master and his staff rose over them, shouting at them to shut up. Farley's head was spinning, darkness popping in front of his eyes like black fireworks. He forced himself to sit up despite the pain in his head, just in time to see two burly men running toward him.

"It was him!" shouted Crowther, rising from the bench, a

giant finger pointed accusingly at Farley. "He struck me!" He turned to the other men at the table. "You all saw it."

Nobody dared to contradict the furious giant. Farley struggled to get up, but he was spared the trouble when the two men seized his arms, yanking him roughly to his feet.

"I'm not surprised," growled one of them. "Always the troublemaker, aren't you?"

His companion snorted. "Another few days in the refractory ward ought to sort you out."

Farley's heart sank. The dank, cold, lonely ward was soul-sapping, just another reason why he hated this workhouse and everyone in it. He allowed himself to be half escorted, half dragged away, and his dizzy head could think of just one thing:

He had to get out. And he had to find Lena.

꧁꧂

ANDREW WAS SHIVERING AS HE TRIED TO WRAP HIS threadbare coat a little tighter around his gaunt little body. He had hardly grown in the past year, and his coat had been too small for him even then; now it was barely able to stretch around his body frame. He gave up on the attempt, plunging his blue fingers into his pockets instead.

"Why do we have to stay out even longer to beg around Christmas?" he asked, his plaintive voice as thin and tremulous as the cold breeze that fingered the back of Lena's neck. "It's the coldest time of year."

Lena sighed. "People have looser purse strings around Christmastime," she said. "They end up giving us more money." She squeezed the hands of the two even smaller children who walked one on each side of her, silent in their cold and exhaustion.

"But what do Judas and Auntie D do with that money?" asked Andrew. "I thought you could buy food with money."

"Of course, you can, Andy," said Lena.

"But then why do we still get just one spoonful of gruel every night?" Andrew turned his big eyes on her, and they seemed deeper than ever in his pinched little face. "If they have more money, why can't we have more food? We have to work so much more at this time of year."

"Yes, Lena," one of the tiny children said, gazing up at her. "Why can't we have more food? We're so hungry."

Lena sighed. She bent down to scoop the child up, planting him on her hip. "I don't know, darling," she said, her heart heavy. "I just don't know."

The children fell silent, too exhausted to speak, and Lena was grateful that their questions had ceased. She led them down the street to the big house where Delilah and Judas were staying. They had no servants, but there was a servant's entrance; Lena used it, sneaking in through the back way as she'd been told to do on pain of a whipping. She led the children toward the back staircase leading up to the top floor where they all slept while Judas and Delilah caroused downstairs.

"You!" Judas's voice barked as Lena passed the door to the drawing room.

She cowered instinctively, expecting a blow. Turning to shield the child on her hip, she didn't dare look up. But no impact came. Instead, there was something dangerously pleased in Judas's voice. "Send the little ones up to their room. You come in here."

Lena looked up. Judas and Delilah were sitting in armchairs opposite each other by the hearth, and there was an opportunistic glitter in Judas's eye she didn't like. But she had no choice except to obey. Setting the child down, she placed his hand in Andrew's.

"Go to your room quietly," she told them. "I'll be right behind you."

"Lena..." Andrew began.

"I told you to go," Lena hissed.

The children turned and bolted up the stairs as fast as their short legs could carry them. Bracing herself, Lena turned and marched into the drawing room.

That was when she spotted her. A tiny heap of pale green silk, cowering by the hearth, the little girl looked up as Lena came in. Her deep brown eyes were filled with tears, her plump, pink cheeks streaked with stains, and she was trembling visibly. Lena felt as though her heart was ripped clean out of her chest by the sight of that little girl with the bonny green ribbons in her hair. She rushed forward, forgetting all about Judas, and snatched the child up into her arms.

"What have you done?" she cried, wheeling around to face him.

Judas was in a good mood. He leaned back in his chair, letting out a lazy laugh. "Be careful with that one, now," he said. "She's going to make us a lot of money."

Lena cradled the child to her chest. The little girl had buried her face in Lena's neck, and she was crying, wholehearted sobs that Lena knew all too well. She stroked her washed and brushed brown hair, her heart pounding.

"This isn't a street child," she gasped.

"No, she's not," said Delilah. Her aged face was contorted into a smug grin. "If she was a street child, she wouldn't be on the verge of making us very rich."

Lena couldn't believe her ears. This little girl had been stolen from her parents, snatched from a warm, safe home – just like she was. She didn't know much about her family, but she did remember having a big house and a governess and books and toys. Once she'd also had ribbons in her hair and a clean face.

Maybe, this little girl had even had the one thing that Lena never did: someone who loved her.

Someone who loved her enough to want her back.

"Help me," the little girl cried, clinging to Lena's neck. "I want my mama."

"Oh, you'll see your mama again," chortled Judas. "Once she's paid a pretty ransom for you, little one."

Delilah shot him an angry look. "We'll talk about that," she snapped. "Take the child to your room, girl," she added to Lena.

Lena wrapped her arms tightly around the little girl and hurried out of the room, hushing her quietly as she sobbed. As soon as they'd reached the stairs, she leaned in, pressing her lips to the child's ear, whispering the words that she was determined to make true.

"I'm going to get you back to your mama," she whispered. "I promise."

CHAPTER 11

The refractory ward was also known as the Black Hole for a reason.

Farley could see nothing and hadn't been able to see anything for days. He knew that his fellow inmates would never be kept in this tiny, black, airless room for more than a day and a night; he also knew of the special hatred the workhouse staff cherished for him—labelling him an upstart, and now he had lost count of the hours that he had spent in the refractory ward. There was no bed here, just a bucket in the corner to use as a lavatory, but that hardly bothered Farley. He barely slept anyway. He had barely slept in the year since he'd lost the small, warm shape of Lena against his back where he rested on his sleeping pallet in the filthy tenement, or the gentle touch of her hand in his when they slept, a reassurance that he wasn't alone.

He was alone now. Completely, utterly, and undeniably alone. He sat very still in the corner, his eyes closed. There was no reason to keep them open. The darkness was absolute.

Footsteps sounded on the corridor outside, but Farley didn't stir. It was probably just some unlucky staff member coming to slide another tasteless meal into the room, and if he opened his eyes, they would just burn with the light.

The lock clicked, and Farley heard the door swing open, painting his eyelids pink with the light. He waited for the scrape of a tray on the floor. Instead, a gravely voice spoke.

"Come on, then," it said.

Farley opened his eyes, straightening his stiff back. He scrambled to his feet, trying to hide his desperation to get out of this room.

"Am I free already?" he asked, forcing his voice to be casual.

The worker sneered. "Christmas Day, isn't it?" he said. "The Master was feeling charitable."

Farley followed the man out into the grey and silent halls of the workhouse. It seemed to be daytime, but he couldn't hear the usual clink of stones being crushed in the courtyard outside; it would appear that Christmas was a holiday in the workhouse. The man led him into a courtyard and shoved him roughly through the door.

"There you are. Try to wait a few days before getting into a fight," he said disdainfully. He patted his stomach. "Still full from Christmas Eve supper last night."

Farley tried not to sneer at the man's bulging belly. He stepped out into the yard, welcoming even the brittle winter sunshine on his skin. The courtyard was as bare and stripped of comfort as Farley's heart felt; it had a grey stone floor, grey stone walls under a grey sky, filled with grey faces that stared at him without interest. He stretched his limbs, grateful at least for the space. He'd barely been able to extend his arms back in the refractory ward.

The men in Farley's group were sitting around, talking or smoking, and he could feel the air change as he looked around at them. A chill seemed to come over the yard, settling over every person. It lay in their eyes as they turned to stare at him, and he could almost feel the menace rising off them in chilly waves. He could feel goose bumps rising on his skin.

Maybe he had angered the wrong man when he'd stood up to Crowther.

Farley turned to look at the worker who hung around by the doorway, puffing on his pipe. He knew there was a plea in his eyes, but the man simply shrugged. He may be in a courtyard with a large group of other men, but he was just as alone as he'd been in the Black Hole.

When Farley turned back to the crowd, Crowther had risen from his place. It was like watching the rising of a tidal wave: peaceful at first, yet with a hint of overwhelming power, of the force with which it could come crashing down. Farley's entire body screamed for him to take a step back, but he wouldn't let it. He folded his arms, looking up at Crowther with a cheerful smile.

"Hello, chaps!" he said, aware of the group of men gathering around the towering ringleader. "Merry Christmas, eh?"

Crowther's first blow was slow enough that Farley could duck. He dived at Crowther's knees, but when his bony shoulder slammed into them, the man barely flinched. Drawing back a leg, he aimed a kick that crunched into Farley's stomach, sending him spinning across the yard. There was a roar of approval from the other men, and Farley stumbled to his feet, sucking for air through his winded chest.

"Did you want to fight me, boy?" demanded Crowther, raising his two fists. They looked like bunches of bananas. "Then fight me."

Farley's eyes darted back toward the worker, but he was cleaning his fingernails, apparently oblivious to the chaos in the yard. He felt his blood surge in his veins. There was no way that Crowther was going to take him down without a fight.

"You don't have to fight me, you know," Crowther said.

Farley felt his lips draw back from his teeth in something that was more snarl than smile. "Yes," he said softly. "I do."

Then he lunged. Crowther swung his arm in a giant haymaker,

but Farley ducked underneath it, his street-fighting skills making him as quick as a cat. He planted a quick series of blows in the big man's ribs and skipped away before Crowther's sweeping hand could seize him. There was a yell of delight from the crowd. Farley grinned, knowing he was dancing on the clifftop of disaster. Crowther seemed to fade from his sight, replaced with the scrawny form of Judas. "Yes," he whispered. "I do have to fight you."

Crowther thundered toward him, a bull-like bellow of rage escaping his lips and swung again. Farley slipped out of the way, rolled and came up with both fists pummelling into the back of Crowther's knee. He gave a howl of pain and fell to one knee, and Farley drew back an arm, ready to deliver justice for that old man, for Andrew, for Lena—

"Get him!" screamed Crowther.

The crowd surged forward, and Farley hesitated, seeing death in their eyes. At that moment, the worker finally raised his voice.

"Oy!" he yelled. "Stop!"

Wary of the Black Hole, the men hesitated. Pushing himself off the doorframe, the worker slouched toward them. Farley was relieved that the worker had come to his rescue, but the look in the man's eyes told him otherwise.

"I think I've seen enough." The worker grabbed Farley's arm, his grip as cold and tight as an iron shackle. "You're a troublemaker. You always will be. And I won't have troublemakers in my workhouse." He sneered. "You can starve on the streets, if that's what you want."

Farley glanced back at the legion of angry men glaring back at him. He looked at the worker, forcing himself to hide the fear behind his eyes.

"It would be better than this," he snapped, and spat on the floor.

He knew the worker's slap was coming, but it still stung across his cheekbone enough that he stumbled a little as the man dragged him away – out of the workhouse, and into the decorated streets of London at Christmas.

⚜

LENA AND THE OTHERS KNEW BETTER THAN TO DO anything except stand very still in the hallway, waiting. Lena was doing her best to hide her nervousness from the other children. Cradling the new little girl – her name was Emily, she said – on her hip, Lena wondered why Judas and Delilah were taking so long. Normally, at this time of year, by the time the children emerged from their room, the couple had made their plans and sent them out onto the streets as early as possible.

But not today. When Lena had led the children down the steps and along the dank hallway to the study, the bigger, airier room was still closed. They'd been waiting for a few minutes now, and as Lena stroked Emily's hair in a bid to soothe her, she could hear Judas and Delilah talking behind the door. Their voices were too low to make out the words, but Lena could tell that they were arguing.

"What's taking so long, Lena?" asked Andrew.

Lena looked down at the little boy hanging on to her hand. "I don't know," she said. "Just be quiet, love. We don't want to make them angry."

By the sound of it, Judas was already angry. Suddenly, he raised his voice, and Lena could make out the words easily enough. "I'm telling you, Delilah, that reward could change our lives! We have enough children to do the begging and stealing for now."

"For now, yes!" Delilah yelled back. "But what about later? You know that Bess is getting too big for this. That's the whole reason we bought Emily."

"Delilah, when we bought Emily for begging, we had no idea about the enormous reward that her parents would offer for her return," Judas shot back. "That little girl is worth a fortune!"

"Especially on the streets! Look how beautiful she is. She'll make far more money over the next few years begging than any silly reward."

Lena cupped a hand against Emily's head, letting her hide her

face in her neck. She didn't want the little one to hear this ugly fight over her fate – a fight that was making rage boil in Lena's own gut even as she listened. Something else was in her stomach at the same time, too: something old and deep, squeezing her very bones.

It was the wish that Lena had what Emily had. A family that cared enough for her to put out a reward. Maybe then, Lena would have grown up safe and sound in her parent's arms instead of cold and starving with this miserable couple.

"Silly? I don't think that kind of money is *silly*, Delilah," snapped Judas. "Lena could teach any child to beg well. Let's claim that reward and buy another one. You know it's the right decision."

"I don't," said Delilah primly. "Because last time, we made the opposite decision. And it was the right one."

Lena frowned. *What are they talking about?*

"What do you mean, woman?" roared Judas.

"I mean that the reward for Lena's return was even bigger," said Delilah, "but keeping her was the right choice. She's made us plenty of money."

Delilah went on, but Lena didn't hear a word of what she said next. She felt as though she'd just been kicked in the chest or had a bucket of ice water thrown in her face. She struggled for breath, winded by the weight of what she had just heard.

The reward for Lena's return was even bigger. There had been a reward put out for her. Her family had searched for her, had cared about her. All the years she'd believed that they simply didn't miss her – they must be a lie. They had to be, if her family, too, had tried to find her.

"Lena? What's wrong?" Emily sat up in Lena's arms, her eyes wide and worried.

Lena couldn't see her own face, but it felt numb and bloodless. She knew she must be pale. Her hands were shaking as she pressed Emily's face back into her shoulder. "Nothing, dear," she said. "Nothing."

No, nothing was wrong. The tattoo her heart was beating against her ribs – *My parents wanted me. My parents wanted me!* – was anything but wrong.

In fact, for the first time since Lena could remember, things felt right. She could feel herself trembling as she hugged Emily even closer. "Your mama and papa are looking for you, honey," she whispered. "And I'm going to make sure that we both fly home."

Now that I know I've got a nest to fly back to.

EMILY WAS SHAKING LIKE A LEAF. LENA TOOK DEEP breaths, trying to steady herself as much as the little girl. The street corner they were standing on looked familiar enough, yet Lena felt as though she were seeing it for the first time. She felt as though she were seeing everything for the first time. It was not the world that was new; it was something inside of her, something that had been utterly transformed by the knowledge that she hadn't been abandoned, after all.

Her family had been searching for her.

She turned her most pleading eyes on an older lady shuffling by with a walking stick, nudging Emily, who held out a tin cup. The little girl didn't have to make an effort to seem pitiful; a night's worth of crying had left her worn-out little face looking as starved as Andrew's.

"Alms?" she croaked. "Alms for the poor?"

"Ah, you poor little angel." The old woman shuffled to a halt. Laboriously, she started to take out her purse. "What a terrible time to be out on the streets."

Emily opened her mouth to speak, but Lena squeezed her hand gently, silencing her. She wasn't watching as coins rattled in the tin cup. Instead, she stole a glance around the intersection where they were standing. It was a crossroads; one path led into the suburbs where Judas and Delilah had been keeping them, and the other was a larger, busier road heading off into the rest of the city. It was wide and open, but busy. Maybe, they'd have a chance – if Lena moved quickly enough.

As far as plans went, there wasn't much to it. Lena had vague ideas about going to a police station or looking through a newspaper for news about Emily and the reward for her. But finding Emily's parents would be easy compared to the monumental task ahead of her: getting away from Judas and Delilah.

"Th-thank you, ma'am," whispered Emily.

Lena forced her attention back to the old woman, who was giving Emily a pitying smile. "Such a lovely thing," she sighed, then began to hobble off. Emily looked up at Lena, her eyes filled with tears. "Why are we doing this?" she pleaded.

Lena put a hand on Emily's shoulder. "Darling, I need you to be as calm as you can," she said. "Just keep doing what I told you – it's going to be over soon."

"Really?" Emily whispered.

Lena's gut twisted. She didn't know the answer to that question. "I need you to trust me," she whispered back, touching Emily's cheek. "I need you to be brave. Can you do that for me? Please?"

Emily's eyes looked utterly lost. "I'll try."

"Good girl." Lena struggled to smile back at her. Straightening, she pretended to scan through the crowd for another target, but instead her eyes rested on where Judas and Delilah were hiding behind a brewer's dray and watching the children. Judas's glittering gaze was on Lena and Emily, and she looked away quickly, her heart thumping so hard that it hurt.

Oh, Farley, where are you? she called in her heart. Farley would know what to do. He was so much braver than she was.

But he wasn't here now, and Lena knew she couldn't let her longing for him distract her, not now. She kept an eye on the crowd, her grip tightening on Emily's hand as she watched Judas out of the corner of her eye. As soon as he looked away...

There! Across the street, a tinker dropped an armful of pots and pans, and the clatter drew Judas's attention. Lena grabbed Emily's hand. "Come on!" she hissed. "Run!"

Emily didn't need telling twice. As Lena lurched off into the crowd, the little girl was right behind her, little whimpers of terror forced from her chest as she bolted. Lena didn't look back at her or at Judas. She kept her eyes forward, clinging to Emily's hand, rushing straight out into the traffic. Voices yelled; Lena heard hooves clattering, cartwheels skidding across the pavement, but there was no time to worry. There was only time to run, and run she did, as fast as she could, as hard as she could, her heart feeling like it was going to rip itself clean out of her chest.

She spotted a gap between two carts and threw herself at it, ignoring a scream of terror from little Emily as she did so. Sparks struck her skirt from a cartwheel, a horse's hot breath huffed on her face, but she ducked under its neck. The side-walk was right in front of her. One last push and she and

Emily could make it. They might just get away. It might just work—

"Got you!" roared a hated, triumphant voice. Lena dodged instinctively, her limbs wild with terror at the sound of Judas's voice, but it was too late. Something small and hard rapped across Lena's shins, and she went down with her full weight. Emily screamed, her hand slipping out of Lena's, and she landed heavily with her shoulder on the edge of the curb.

"Emily!" Lena cried, rolling over as quickly as she could. Her world was a scramble of grey sky and frightened faces, and Delilah, grabbing Emily's arm, her fingernails digging into the child's skin.

"Let her go!" Lena shouted, scrambling to her feet.

"You mangy dog!" Judas bellowed, seizing Lena's throat. His eyes were wild. "Did you really think you could get away from me?"

Lena spat the words, squeezing them out past his iron grip. "I will get away from you."

She drew up her legs as high as she could and planted both feet in his groin. He gave a catlike yowl of anger and pain, and his grip loosened on her neck. Lena landed on her hands and knees and then her feet. She scrambled to move, hearing cries of surprise and horror around her. Her feet wanted to flee, but her heart forced her to stay. Delilah was dragging Emily into the crowd.

"Lena!" Emily screamed. "LENA!"

"Emily!" Lena yelled, starting toward her.

But Judas was already back on his feet and coming at her. Lena ducked a wild blow from his fist, but she didn't see the other fist coming, and it slammed into her cheekbone, making stars explode in front of her eyes. She staggered back, fell to the dirt, and then he was on top of her, his knees straddling her, the scent of his awful tobacco filling her world as his fists hammered into her shoulders, her face, her ribs. Pain filled her world like a red mist, and she could only dimly hear Emily's screams fading into the distance.

"Get off her!" voices were shouting. "Let her go!"

The blows stopped. Lena struggled to open her eyes. A group of men had seized Judas's arms; she could hear police whistles in the distance, but Judas's teeth were bared, his eyes still wild with rage as he lunged against his captors. She forced herself to her feet despite her spinning head, mopping blood from her cheeks.

"Where are you going to run to?" Judas spat, struggling against the men that held him.

Lena took a step closer, feeling her veins fill with fire. "To the family that still wants me," she snapped.

Judas roared. He dragged himself free of the men and lunged at her, and Lena could think of only one thing to do. She ran.

CHAPTER 12

The two little girls by the fire could not have been more different. Joan took another little sip of her cup of eggnog, watching as they sat side-by-side on the hearth rug, both gently brushing their dolls' hair. Seraphine, the eldest, had pitch-black hair like her father's, and also his piercing blue eyes. Her long, black hair poured down her back, glossy and beautiful.

The settee creaked as Charles sat down beside her, offering a tender smile. He laid a hand on her knee and a kiss on her cheek. "Merry Christmas, my love."

Joan made herself smile, returning the kiss. She glanced up at the towering Christmas tree in the corner of the room. Some of the gingerbread figures were a little misshapen, but she knew the little girls had loved helping her make them. The brightly coloured baubles and tinsel wrapped around the tree reminded her that this was supposed to be a happy time of year.

"They're so beautiful," Charles murmured, looking at the two little girls. He put an arm around her shoulders. "I can't believe that Seraphine is seven years old already."

"And Patricia, five," said Joan. "The time has gone by so quickly."

"That's true." Charles squeezed Joan's shoulders. "You three are all a gift to me, my love."

Joan smiled as well as she could, her heart cracking. *We should have been four.*

"Mama!" Patricia got up from the hearth, hurrying over to Joan. She laid her small hands on Joan's. "Can I have a rocking-horse for Christmas?"

"You already have a rocking-horse, darling," said Charles, with a deep, beautiful chuckle.

"But Seraphine says he was her rocking-horse first." Patricia poked out her pink bottom lip, cuddling her dolly to her chest. "Oh, please, Papa, may I have one all my own?"

Joan could see Charles's heart melting, and she couldn't blame him. She couldn't say no to those bright blue eyes any more than he could. They reminded her so much of... *No.* She didn't want to think the name. She was supposed to be happy.

Charles smiled, reaching out to touch the tip of Patricia's nose. "I suppose I could speak to Father Christmas for you."

Patricia's blue eyes lit up. She laughed, bouncing in place, her rich golden curls soft on her shoulders. "Thank you, Papa!" She ran to Seraphine, grabbing her sister's hand. "Come on, Sera – let's go and play on the rocking-horse. I need to practice so that I can ride mine in the big race."

Seraphine giggled. "Let's go!"

Joan managed to wait until both of the little girls had made it out of the room and into the nursery before the first tear spilled down her cheek. She clapped a hand over her mouth, trying her best to hold back a sob.

"Joanie!" Charles wrapped his arms around her, planting kisses on her hands, her forehead. "Oh, Joanie, my love."

"I'm sorry, Charles," Joan cried. "I'm trying not to spoil Christmas – I really am."

"And you're being so brave." Charles cuddled her closer.

"Christmas has just never been the same," Joan whispered, looking up at him.

She saw the agony in his blue eyes. "Nothing has ever been the same," he whispered. He pulled her almost into his lap, pressing his lips to her hair.

"It's been eight years, Charles," Joan whispered. "Eight years, and still I miss her every single day. Patricia looks so much like her, sometimes it breaks my heart to see her."

"I know," said Charles. "Patricia is a gift, and so is Seraphine. But somehow..." He gave a deep sigh, a breath of agony from the very centre of his soul. "Our family has never felt complete since Lena died."

"I miss her so much," said Joan.

"I miss her, too, darling," said Charles. He swallowed hard, and Joan knew he was trying to hold back his own tears. "I miss her, too."

❧

LENA BENT OVER THE PUDDLE, DIPPED THE CORNER OF HER dress in the foul water, and patted it across her swollen cheek. Some of the dry blood washed off, staining the white hem pink. She paused, peering into the reflection in the puddle, and grimaced. Even with the blood washed off, her face was still purple and yellow and deep blue. Maybe that was why every person who'd answered the doors she'd knocked on tonight had chased her away.

Getting to her feet, Lena pushed her hair back, trying her best to hold on to her resolve. It was dark now, and the chill was coming in with the snowflakes that drifted down all around her. The street that she was walking through was quiet, although she could hear bursts of merriment from behind the windows of the pretty houses that she passed; there were families feasting together behind every window, and Lena realized that today must be Christmas. For the first time this season, she felt as though that meant something. As though Christmas might be for her, too, even though Farley wasn't there to make it merry.

A gentleman hurrying along the street gave her a wary, side-long glance, as if trying to decide whether or not she was worth the effort of kicking. Lena quickly tugged at her hair, loosening some of her blonde curls and allowing them to fall over her swollen face. The cold nipped at her bruises, making them ache all the more. Christmas or no, she realized that the cold was growing deadly. She had so many people to find – Mama, Papa, Farley. She hoped that they were still out there. But for right now, she would have to get somewhere safe to sleep first.

She tried the servant's entrance of the next house, rapping on the doorway hopefully. Christmastime must be busy for servants of houses like this; surely, they'd be grateful for a helping hand. When the door was yanked open, Lena gazed up at an old woman with a face like an old leather shoe.

"Good evening, ma'am," she said, as cheerfully as she could, widening her blue eyes the way she knew was captivating. "I was..."

"Go away!" snapped the housekeeper, slamming the door.

Lena stared at the wood, feeling her heart sink. It seemed that life without Judas and Delilah might not only be hard.

Judging by the rising cold, it could also be short.

MANY HOURS AND COUNTLESS SLAMMED DOORS LATER, THE spark that had burned so deeply in Lena's heart seemed to be extinguished. She wanted nothing more than to lie down and rest, but she knew that in this cold, stillness was death. She'd seen enough frozen corpses to be aware of that fact. One of them from a child that Judas and Delilah had thrown onto the streets earlier.

She tried not to think of his stiff and frozen face, captured in his last contortion of pain and fear, dragging herself up the path to yet another stately home where the people inside were warm and well-fed and happy and together. The way her family had been, before Judas and Delilah. She vaguely remembered a housemaid – *Ella*. She had been the one who had taken her away from home. Lena tried to be angry, but all she could feel was cold and exhausted.

She had started out asking every housekeeper she saw if there was a position for her. Then she had started to ask for just an evening's work, and now she was reduced to begging, the only thing she was good at. Trembling, she reached the narrow servant's entrance, raised a fist and knocked on the door. Her knuckles were too numb to feel the wood, but she heard it echo inside.

The door opened. A burst of light fell on Lena, and she held up a hand against it, blinking. Warmth came with it, and a delicious, hearty smell – something cooking. It made her stomach burn.

"Yes, yes, what do you want?" a voice demanded.

Lena lowered her hand, blinking, and looked into a pair of sharp brown eyes. She tucked her hair over her bruised cheek and found her best smile. "I'm sorry to bother you, ma'am," she simpered. "It's terribly cold out tonight. I was wondering..."

She stopped, struck by the housekeeper's expression. The woman had streaks of iron grey in her hair, which was pulled back neatly into a bun, but those streaks seemed colourful in comparison with her ashen face. The colour seemed to have been sucked out of it, and her eyes were wide with utter shock. She looked as though a dead body had risen from the grave in front of her, her expression so petrified that the hairs rose on the back of Lena's own neck.

"Wh-what is it?" Lena stammered, shaken. She glanced over her shoulder, half expecting to see some ghoulish apparition behind her.

"Why are you here?" the housekeeper croaked, still staring at Lena.

She pulled herself together as well as she could. Her aching, trembling knees reminded her that she couldn't walk much further tonight; this housekeeper might be her last chance for survival this Christmas.

"Ma'am, I don't mean to intrude," she whispered, widening her eyes. "I – I'm just down on my luck, and I need a place to sleep tonight. Please, ma'am, if I could just curl up in your pantry or your scullery or even in the stables with your horses. Anywhere."

The housekeeper cleared her throat. A little colour seemed to be returning to her cheeks. Lena pushed on, sensing an opening. "I wouldn't ask, but it's Christmas," she said. "Who should starve to death at Christmas?"

"Oh, I can think of plenty," the housekeeper said, her words coming out in a bitter sigh. "But it isn't you." She glanced over her shoulder. "Come on – quick now. Don't let anyone see you."

Lena could hardly believe it. She didn't wait for the house-keeper to change her mind. Scurrying through the door, she felt a welcome warmth wash over her as the housekeeper quickly closed the door behind her. A bony claw landed on her shoulder, and the woman glanced around worriedly, but the group of people sitting around the fire in the kitchen hadn't looked up.

"Come on," she hissed. "Quietly."

Tiptoeing around Judas and Delilah all her life had made Lena good at sneaking. She pattered soundlessly beside the housekeeper, following her as she paused for a second by the kitchen table and then moved quickly down a few stone steps into a dark cellar. The housekeeper lit a candle, holding it up to reveal a tiny, empty, dusty space.

"It's bare, but it'll be warm," she said. Hesitating, she reached into her pocket, drawing out a bun that she must have taken from the kitchen table when she'd paused there. "Here," she grunted.

Lena could hardly believe her eyes. She took the bun reverently; it was so fresh it nearly fell apart her hands, and the scent of it was like a piece of heaven.

"Oh, thank you," she gasped breathlessly. "Thank you. Thank you!" She couldn't help it. She threw her arms around the housekeeper's waist, clinging to her. "I don't know how to thank you."

The housekeeper froze, stiff as an ironing board. She put a hand on Lena's shoulder, gently pushing her back.

"Be quiet down here. And be gone in the morning," she said quickly.

Lena nodded eagerly. "Yes, ma'am. Of course, ma'am."

"Good." The housekeeper put the candle down on a niche and turned to hurry back up the steps. She paused halfway up, turning back. "Ah..."

Lena looked up. "Yes?"

A furrow appeared between the housekeeper's eyes, and she shook her head. "Never mind."

With that, the door clanked shut, and the housekeeper was gone. Exhausted and grateful beyond description, Lena sank to the ground, pressing the warm bun to her nose to inhale its divine scent. It was just a plain bit of bread, and the cellar was just a cold black box, but at that moment, it was the first Christmas where any real hope had ever filled her heart.

❧

THE HOUSEKEEPER TOOK HER PLACE AGAIN BY THE FIRE, HER heart beating in a hundred different places all over her body. What had she just seen? How could it be true?

"Are you all right?" asked a kitchen maid, her face aglow with merriment and the brandy she held in her hand. She laid a hand on the housekeeper's arm. "You look like you've seen a ghost."

The housekeeper managed a smile. "Just a little stomach ache, that's all."

"Here!" The stable boy laughed, pouring her a stiff glass of brandy. "This will make you feel better."

He held it out to her, and the housekeeper didn't argue. She took it and knocked back a solid gulp, feeling that she needed it.

"Easy there," said the stable boy. "The night is but a pup."

The butler laughed. "And you aren't anymore." He smiled and spoke her name. "Ella."

FARLEY COULDN'T BELIEVE THAT HE HAD FOUND IT.

He stood at the end of the street for a long moment, his heart hammering against his ribs like the wings of a caged bird determined to break free. It was right there in front of him, just as he had left it: a tumbledown tenement, the same door that he'd run through in a bid to save Rodney, the wall that Judas had pinned him up against—the very same walls in which he'd sung Christmas carols with Andrew, the broken windowpane that had let in the icy wind one year ago when he'd lain on his sleeping pallet with an arm around Lena's bony little body. The place where Judas and Delilah lived with the children.

The place where he wound finally find Lena.

His legs were trembling with weakness and hunger as he stepped forward. If it wasn't for the fact that he was about to see the only person he'd ever had to love, he would gladly have exchanged the blackness of the refractory ward for the desolation of London streets in winter. But Lena made all the difference, the way she always had ever since she was just a tiny child, and Farley had first set eyes on her eight years before. His feet gained momentum. The next thing he knew, he was jogging. Then running. Not caring about Judas or Delilah or whoever else might hear him. Just ready to see Lena's face. Just to be able to hold her—

He launched himself up the last two steps, planted his feet on the landing and grabbed the door handle. Now, this very second, she was going to run out into his arms. She was going to throw herself into his embrace at last.

"Lena!" he cried and pulled the door open.

His voice echoed around the empty room. There were no pallets on the floor. Not even a scrap of blanket, nothing but the bare, splintery boards. Dust on the windowsill. Snow on the floor. Cobwebs in the corner, catching snowflakes. No Andrew. No Judas or Delilah. And certainly, awfully, no Lena.

Farley's legs gave up. He crumpled to the ground, his face buried in his hands, the sobs bubbling up from somewhere deep in his guts to burst damply across his face. Of course, she wasn't here. Judas and Delilah never stayed in one place for long; they must have moved the children somewhere else. And where that could be, he could not begin to guess.

He had to scream something. So he screamed her name, an animal cry of loneliness and heartache, launched into the abyss that her absence had left in his life. And he screamed it again, and again and again, and only the silence answered.

PART III

CHAPTER 13

Four Years Later

"ALMS?" ANDREW HELD UP THE TIN CUP, HIS DARK EYES turned up toward the muffled crowd that bustled past him. "Alms?" He rattled the two coins within; they made a lonely little noise, chinking hopelessly against one another. "Alms for the hungry?"

Farley sighed, looking down into his own cup. Andrew was already too big to be adorable enough to tug at the heartstrings of this busy holiday crowd. He hadn't stood a chance himself, and there was only a single penny lying at the bottom of his cup.

"Come on, Andy," he said gently, putting an arm around Andrew's shoulders. "I think it's time to call it a night."

Andrew looked up at Farley, his eyes despondent. "But we can barely buy any supper with this."

"Don't worry. I'm not hungry," Farley lied. "It's getting cold out – let's go and get you something to eat."

Andrew gave him another wary look, but he was still only nine or ten; too little to really argue. Farley took his hand, leading him over to the funny old lady who sold a strange, nameless soup. Farley didn't want to know what was in it – he assumed that whatever meat it contained didn't come from a sheep or a cow; he hoped vaguely it was only horse – but at least it was hot, and judging by the way Andrew slurped it down, it was good enough.

"Here," Andrew said, following closely as they headed back to the alleyway where they slept. He held up the cup, which was only half empty. Despite the hunger in his eyes, Andrew pushed it against Farley. "You can have the rest."

Farley's stomach knotted, but he smiled, pushing the cup away. "Finish it. It's all right."

Andrew took another, reluctant sip, and Farley saw the despair in his eyes.

"Don't worry, Andy," he said. "It's only two weeks to go until Christmas. We've been doing this for nearly four years together, just you and me. I still am grateful I found you on the street. That was lucky, don't you think? And you know that we have a better time at Christmas now that Judas and Delilah aren't taking all our earnings."

"That's true," said Andrew. He sighed deeply. "That last Christmas with them was the most terrifying time of my whole life."

Farley shook his head, his heart filling with regret. "I'm still sorry that I wasn't there." Anger filled his voice. "I should have been there."

"You would have been proud," said Andrew. "Lena was so brave – just like you. Or maybe braver. Judas was going to kill her, but she stood up to him all the same while Delilah was dragging Emily away."

Farley closed his eyes, trying not to imagine Judas's cruel fists punching into Lena's beautiful, sweet face. "Why would anyone want to hurt her like that?" he growled.

"She was trying to save Emily, remember?" said Andrew. "And she did, too. With all the commotion she made fighting Judas, Lena made the whole street angry with him. They saw him hitting her, and they grabbed him until the coppers got there."

"And so Emily was taken back to her parents." Farley sighed. "Why did Lena run, Andrew? If only she'd stayed, maybe the police could have taken her back to her own family."

"She was scared," said Andrew. He shrugged. "I was scared,

too. I did just the same as she did and ran. I didn't know that the police wanted to help; Judas and Delilah always told us that they'd eat us or feed us to savage dogs, remember?"

"I do remember," said Farley. "It took me a long time to explain to you what we'd read in the papers – that the police had rescued Emily."

"So maybe Lena was afraid of them, too," said Andrew. "Maybe she ran because she didn't know what else to do."

"I wish I knew which way she went," said Farley. If only she had stayed with Andrew—he would have found her, too. The ache in his heart for her was sometimes more than he could bear. His voice was quiet, speaking almost to himself instead of to the little boy. "I wish I could find her."

They had reached the alleyway, and Andrew was quiet as they stepped into the little corner that Farley had tried to partition off with old barrels and a rag hanging on a piece of string between the walls. Still sipping at his soup, Andrew sat in a corner with his back to the wall while Farley tried to light their last two bits of firewood.

He tried to strike a match on the ground, but it was damp. Frowning, Farley looked inside their matchbox. There were only two matches left.

"Farley?" Andrew whispered.

Farley looked up. "What is it?" he asked.

"Do you... you know..." Andrew paused. "Do you really think you'll find her?"

"Lena?" Farley tried to smile, even though Andrew's words awoke his deepest fear. He put down the matchbox for the time being and sat down next to the little boy, putting his arm around the bony frame. "Of course, I do."

"But why?" Andrew's face was desperate and solemn. "I know what would have happened to me if you hadn't found me."

Farley tucked Andrew closer into his arms. He didn't want to think about the truth of the little boy's words. When Farley had seen the piece in the paper about Emily's return to her parents, he'd known in his heart that Judas and Delilah were involved and made his way to the street where the arrest had taken place.

"It hurt so bad when I broke my ankle running away from them," said Andrew, rubbing the place on his leg that still ached in the cold. "But it was lucky, I guess. It was the only reason that I was still close enough to where they'd been arrested for you to find me."

"And you were half-starved." Farley sighed. "But Lena is strong, Andrew. She must have made her way somewhere safe."

"Where would be safe for her?" Andrew asked. "Where could she go?"

Farley's gut felt like it was being squeezed. He knew that

there was almost nowhere in this city where an unwanted young girl could safely go. Had she ended up in the clutches of someone even worse than Judas and Delilah, someone who'd noticed her beautiful little figure? Or had she gone, in desperation, to a workhouse? The awfulness of that place had nearly killed Farley; he couldn't bear to imagine what it would do to Lena.

"We'll find her, Andrew," said Farley, trying to summon a hope he didn't feel. "Somehow, we'll still find her."

Andrew leaned his head against Farley's shoulder. "I suppose we can't go to the country, then."

"The country?" Farley drew back, looking at him. "What are you talking about?"

"One of the boys at the market with his family today was talking about it," said Andrew. "He said there's lots of food in the country and even jobs. I thought we could go there."

Farley stroked Andrew's hair, trying to formulate an answer. The idea of leaving London – which felt, for all its opulence and bustle, like a great and barren desert after four years on its streets – had occurred to him before. But one thing had kept him here. One thing that he couldn't shake.

"We will go, one day," he said. "After we've found Lena."

Andrew knew better than to argue. Because even five years after he'd last set eyes on Lena, that flame in Farley's soul had never been quenched.

LENA STARED AT THE MUFFLED FIGURE HURRYING BY ON THE street. He was lanky and slender, and something about his shape was familiar in a way that made her heart speed up. She squinted against the swirl of snowflakes, trying to make out the man's face, but it was muffled in a scarf. Maybe, when he passed, she could glimpse his hair. And if he had wheaten curls, then...

He didn't. As he turned to hail a cab, Lena caught a glimpse of short, black hair. She sighed, stepping back. It wasn't Farley. All the times she'd stared out of the window of her mistress's hat shop, it had never been Farley. Yet she couldn't stop herself from staring.

"Lena?" The gentle voice prompted her out of her reverie. She turned quickly, finding a smile. "Sorry, Mrs. Weston," she said. "I was lost in thought."

Mrs. Weston laughed, making pleasant dimples in her plump cheeks. "Aren't we all, at your age?" she said wistfully. "I do beg your pardon, ma'am," she said to her customer.

The customer gazing into the mirror gave a good-natured smile. "We were all sixteen once, you know," she said.

Lena felt a blush heating up her cheeks. She cleared her throat, handing the hat in her hands over to the customer. "I think this might be more your colour, ma'am."

The lady settled the extravagant touring hat on her head and smiled, touching its lacy edges. "Why, you have a lovely eye, young lady," she said. "Navy has never been my favourite colour, but it seems to rather suit me."

"It suits you beautifully, ma'am," said Mrs. Weston with a smile. Her eyes met Lena's in the mirror. "It's just the thing for your holiday in the country."

Lena returned Mrs. Weston's smile in the mirror, her heart thumping with gratitude. There was movement behind her, and she turned as a young man entered the shop.

"Mother, are you finally done?" he asked, in tones of elegant boredom. "I've finished up my holiday shopping, and it really is time to go home now."

"Now, now, Patrick," said the lady, her voice chiding. "I've nearly made my choice. Do try to be patient."

But Patrick had already forgotten his boredom. Lena saw a familiar look creep into his eyes as he looked her up and down, starting at the hem of her plain blue dress and traveling up her growing curves to her face. By the time his eyes met hers, the expression was unmistakable: it was a cross between drooling hunger and hunter's focus, and it made a cold shiver run down her spine. She averted her eyes quickly, moving behind Mrs. Weston.

"Can I put this in a box for you, ma'am?" she asked, her voice trembling.

"Yes, I do think so," said the lady. She took off the hat and handed it to Lena. "Thank you."

Lena retreated back behind the counter. Mrs. Weston, mercifully, had noticed the young man's expression. She kept her dumpy little old figure between Patrick and Lena until Lena could hand the hat box to the older lady and the pair of them had left. Patrick gave a last, hungry glance over his shoulder. As soon as the door had closed behind them, Lena slumped onto the counter, breathing a sigh of relief.

"Oh, Mrs. Weston," she said. "Thank you."

Mrs. Weston laughed. "It's nothing, my dear." She patted Lena's back.

"No, it's not." Lena looked up, her lips curving into a grateful smile. "I have never been more desperate than the day that I came to your door, begging for a job. I half believed that you weren't going to give it to me – just like all of the other people I'd been asking for days. But you did, and it took me off the streets." She shivered, wrapping her arms around her body. "When I was little, I always thought that things would get easier as I got older. But they only got harder out there."

Mrs. Weston clasped Lena's shoulder, her smile growing misty. "I had a daughter just like you, Lena. A beautiful, sweet, gentle child. She was about your age when the consumption took her." She tucked a lock of Lena's golden hair behind her ear. "You were a little Christmas blessing to me."

"And you, to me," said Lena. "Thank you."

"I just wish I could pay you better," said Mrs. Weston.

Lena laughed. "Oh, no, Mrs. Weston. Don't say that," she said. "Consider your protection from Patrick's wandering eye to be my Christmas bonus."

Mrs. Weston gave a merry, bubbling laugh, a sound so infectious that Lena had to join in even though the disappointment of the young man out there on the street – the man who had proven not to be Farley – was still a crushing blow. Not for the first time, she thanked God in her heart for leading her to Mrs. Weston's doorstep. The old lady was poor, and the hours were long, but at least she knew she was safe in the hat shop.

"Well, my dear, one day you'll find a man who looks at you differently." Mrs. Weston smiled as she started to rearrange the spools of hat ribbon by the counter.

"What do you mean?" asked Lena.

"Not all men are like young Patrick back there," said Mrs. Weston. She turned to Lena, the kindly wrinkles beside her eyes crinkling like a sweet wrapper. "One day, you'll come across a young man who doesn't look at you like you're a tasty meal – but like you're a priceless jewel."

A priceless jewel. Lena felt a smile tug at her lips, even though her heart was filled with longing and sorrow. "I think I know what you mean," she whispered.

"Oh?" Mrs. Weston's eyes sparkled. "Do tell, darling! Did you meet someone in church perhaps?"

"No, no. It's not like that." Lena sucked in a breath. "He's from... before. Before you took me in."

Mrs. Weston raised an eyebrow. "But you were only twelve years old then, my dear."

"I know, and he was just a friend to me," said Lena, "but he was the greatest friend I could ever have hoped for. He was the only hope I had back with..." She shuddered. "*Them.*"

Something dark flashed through Mrs. Weston's eyes at the mention of Judas and Delilah. "Was he kidnapped, too?"

"He couldn't remember. All he knew was living with that couple," said Lena. "He has hair the colour of wheat in a field, and soft grey eyes, and a scar just here." She traced a finger down her cheek. "They cut him to make him look more pitiful for the begging. He'd suffered so much, ma'am. But he was a friend to me when nobody else was."

"What happened to him?" asked Mrs. Weston.

"He disappeared." Lena swallowed, remembering the pain of that Christmas. "About a year before I escaped. I've searched so hard for him. And I just know that if I could only find him, I would love him forever, the way you loved your Peter."

Mrs. Weston's eyes grew misty at the memory of her late husband. "Oh, Lena," she said, putting an arm around Lena's shoulders. "Love is one of the greatest blessings we can ever have in our lives. I don't want you to miss it."

"Are you saying I should give up on Farley?" Lena asked.

"No, my darling." Mrs. Weston gave her a little squeeze. "I'm saying that you should keep on holding onto hope for a miracle."

Lena laughed. "When you talk like that, Mrs. Weston, it makes me hope that someday I might even find my family again."

"You will," said Mrs. Weston firmly.

"But I've been trying for years, ma'am," said Lena. "I've tried to remember their faces, our home – even my last name." She sighed. "And nothing has worked."

"I know," said Mrs. Weston. "It would take a miracle." She smiled. "But it is Christmastime, after all. It's the season for miracles."

CHAPTER 14

The bell over the door jingled, and gentle giggling filled the shop. Lena smiled, lifting a last hat onto its shelf. It sounded like there were children in the shop – probably looking for either a gift or some mischief to get up to, and either way, they were always more fun than the stuck-up old ladies looking for a fashion statement.

"I'll be right there!" she called, arranging the hat just right on the shelf before climbing down from the stepladder and turning toward the counter. Mrs. Weston was out running an errand, and it was just the two girls with her in the shop. They were beautiful children; one only four or five years younger than Lena, the other a little smaller. The older one had pitch-black hair and luminous blue eyes that danced with merriment.

"Good morning!" she chirped, a grin spreading over her face like a sunrise.

"Hello!" said Lena, laughing. "You two look terribly excited."

"We're ever so excited," said the smaller one. Her eyes were blue like her sister's, but her hair was a shade of richest gold. "We're being terribly brave and clever."

"Are you?" asked Lena, smiling.

"We're going to buy a gift for our mama," said the older one. A note of solemnity crept into her bearing. "I'm eleven years old, you know, and I'm big enough to buy Mama a gift all by myself."

"But with me," added the little one, giggling.

The older girl shook her head. "Unfortunately," she muttered under her breath, and Lena had to stifle a laugh.

"Well, what kind of gift are you looking for?" she asked. The girls had satiny dresses and smartly polished shoes; she knew that they had to come from some rich family.

"Mama wants a hat," stated the small one.

"But not just any kind of hat. Mama's taste is very particular in hats," announced the elder. She tossed her raven hair. "She's going to want one that's just exactly right."

"Luckily for you, I know all about hats," said Lena, with a wink. "What kind of hat would she like? We have teardrop hats and touring hats and boaters and riding hats and bonnets – any kind of hat you can think of."

"Let's get her a bonnet," said the small one, giggling mischievously. "She'll be ever so happy."

"Yes," said the older girl firmly. "But we know that Mama doesn't go outside much, so we won't need a boater or a riding hat."

"What does your mama like to do?" asked Lena.

"Well, she's not very well, so she mostly stays inside," said the older girl. "But she does like to go out and visit friends for dinner."

"Then she'll need something classy and stylish, don't you think?" said Lena. "Come on. Let me show you."

Hand-in-hand, the two little girls followed her over to the display where Mrs. Weston's finest hats stood proudly on the shelves. Lena caressed a pastel pink mini top hat. "What about this?" she said.

"Oh, no," said the smaller girl. "Mama doesn't like pink at all."

"And she doesn't often wear mini hats," the older girl chipped in.

"How about this, then?" asked Lena. She lifted a forest green teardrop hat from the shelf, and the older girl's eyes lit up. She reached out, allowing her fingertips to brush the pretty plumes that adorned it.

"This is beautiful," she breathed. "It would look so wonderful with Mama's pretty hair."

"I love it!" said the smaller one.

Doubt crept into the older girl's eyes. "I don't know if Mama will like it, though," she said.

"Maybe you could bring your mama in to try it on," said Lena. "I know you want to give her a surprise for Christmas, but you can make it an early present. Early presents are lovely, don't you think?" She parroted the line; she herself didn't know a thing about early presents, but Mrs. Weston often said so.

"That's a good idea," said the older girl. "We should surprise Mama with the news and then bring her here to pick out the one she likes."

The younger girl gazed up at Lena, her irresistible blue eyes filled with longing. "Oh, can't I just try one of them on?" she said. "I know I'm too little to have a pretty hat like that, but I just want to see."

Lena smiled. The shop was quiet, and she just couldn't say no to those eyes.

"Of course," she said. "Here." She settled the much-too-big hat on the little girl's head, gripped her shoulders and turned her around to face the mirror. "What do you think?"

The little girl pushed the hat back out of her eyes, nudging it askew on her head, and a gasp ran through the both of them. The little girl's eyes widened, admiring the fancy hat, but it wasn't the hat that had made a strange shock run through Lena's body. Crouching down beside the girl, Lena's eyes were level with hers in the mirror.

And they were exactly the same.

Lena couldn't stop staring. The little girl's eyes were the very same shade of blue as her own; they were the same almond shape, with the same depth of expression. Except hers were now dancing with joy, while Lena knew her own were wide with surprise. Slowly, she reached over her shoulder for a lock of her golden hair and gently laid it on her chest. It was the same colour and style as the rich, bouncing curls on this little girl.

The resemblance was so uncanny that Lena was still staring when the shop door opened, bringing with it a gust of cold wind and a flurry of snowflakes.

"Oh, what a mess!" cried Mrs. Weston cheerfully. Spotting her customers, she chuckled in delight. "Hello, darlings!"

Lena forced herself to her feet, blinking.

"H-hello, Mrs. Weston," she said. She glanced at the mirror one more time, trying to pull herself together. "These little girls just came in to pick out a hat for their mama."

"But we're going to come back later so that Mama can try them on," said the older girl solemnly.

"Well, that's a wonderful idea," said Mrs. Weston.

The little girl took off the green hat and handed it back to Lena. "Thank you," she piped, smiling. "Come on! Let's go and tell Mama all about it," she added, seizing her sister's hand.

"All... all right," said the older girl, her eyes darting up to Lena's. She looked a little shocked herself.

"Come *on*, Seraphine!" cried the little girl, dragging her sister toward the door.

When they were gone, Lena had to sit down, staring at nothing. Mrs. Weston raised her eyebrows. "Are you all right, dear?"

"Y-yes," said Lena. "I suppose I am."

"What lovely little girls!" said Mrs. Weston. "And that smaller one looked just like you." She laughed. "It's a funny old world, isn't it?"

Lena wasn't sure about that. But there was definitely a funny feeling in the pit of her stomach.

CHAPTER 15

It was so good to see Mama outside for once. Her face was pale above her elegant burgundy scarf, but there was a little sparkle in her amber eyes that Seraphine hadn't seen for a long time. She grinned up at her mother, holding her hand and trying to hide the worry in her heart.

"Are you sure you're all right to walk, Mama?" she asked.

"I'm fine, my dear." Mama smiled. "It's time I had a little exercise in the fresh air. It's only a couple of blocks away from home, and it's a lovely day."

"It's so nice that we found a hat shop so close by," Seraphine agreed. "I know we were all sad when the old shop closed down, but now we found such a lovely little place that's not far from us."

Mama laughed pleasantly. "I'll take your word for it, darling."

"It's very nice, Mama," said Patricia, grinning up at their mother as she skipped alongside her. "There are so many very, very beautiful hats."

Seeing the smile on Mama's face was a good feeling. Seraphine allowed herself to relax a little as she strolled along beside her mother, gazing at the festive scene around them. Christmas was only a few days away, and it was a beautiful winter's morning; the sky was pale blue above them, sparkling off the snow that still lay beside the streets.

"I'm glad you liked the hats, Patty," said Mama, laughing at Patricia's excitement.

"They're so pretty, Mama. And there are so many of them! All sorts of shapes and colours and sizes. And the nice girl from the hat shop will help us. She's very kind," said Patricia. "She let me try on one of the hats. I looked awfully grown-up."

Seraphine said nothing, her heart running back to the moment when that girl had crouched down beside Patricia in the mirror. She knew by the widening of the girl's eyes that she'd noticed the same thing that Seraphine did: how much she looked like an older, carbon copy of Patricia, so much so that Seraphine hadn't been able to stop staring. It had been absolutely uncanny. She knew that it was nothing more than a coincidence, yet she couldn't shake the feeling that there was more to the sweet hat shop girl than met the eye.

"There it is, Mama!" Patricia tugged her hand out of Mama's. She pointed excitedly at the little hat shop; Seraphine could just see it at the far end of the other side of the street. "The hat shop!"

"Patricia, stop!" shouted Mama.

But the little girl was much too excited to listen. She ran out into the road, and Seraphine felt her heart stop. There was a clatter of hooves just up the road, and Seraphine whirled around in time to see the milk cart come barreling toward her. It was drawn by two shaggy, wild-eyed mules, and their driver had spotted the little golden head in the road ahead of him a moment too late. He leaned back, hauling on the reins, dragging at the brake, sparks flying from the cartwheels, but the squeal of the brakes had spooked the mules and they were dragging the cart forward over the slippery ice.

"Patty!" Seraphine shrieked, lunging forward.

"Sera, no!" screamed Mama, grabbing her arm.

Patricia heard them at last, but it was already too late. She stopped, turning to stare at the wall of snorting, trampling death that was heading straight toward her. Incomprehension crossed her face, followed by fear. The little girl screamed, and the cart was only feet from her when a figure came flying across the road. Long-limbed, flaxen hair flying, a young man launched himself across the street toward her. Patricia gave a yelp of terror and they tumbled away, and then the cart was charging past, its wheels groaning on the ice, the mules trying to find their way to a halt.

"Patricia!" cried Mama.

The little girl was just a heap of pink silk lying by the curb alongside the figure of the young man, who had one skinny arm draped around her. For a breathless moment, neither of them moved. Then Patricia sat up.

"Mama!" she gasped.

"Patty!" Mama shrieked. Her knees buckled in relief, and Seraphine threw her arms around her mother, trying to keep her from falling to the dirty sidewalk.

"Mama, it's all right," she cried, pulling her close. "She's all right."

"Oh, Patty, Patty," Mama whimpered, tears pouring down her elegant face.

"Ma'am, it's all right," said the young man who was suddenly beside them. Seraphine stared up at him; he was tall and dirty and smelly, but there was a softness in his eyes that made her feel at ease. He had Patricia in his arms, and he thrust her at Mama. "She's not hurt. She's perfectly all right."

Mama almost snatched Patricia from him, and he grabbed her arm, helping her to her feet as she pulled the little girl into her arms.

"Oh, Patty, you naughty, naughty little girl," she gasped, showering kisses on Patricia's cheeks and forehead. "Have I never told you not to run into the road?"

"I'm sorry, Mama," Patricia sobbed. "I was just so excited."

Seraphine grabbed the young man's hand, overwhelmed with relief. "Thank you so much," she gasped.

"Yes − yes. Where are my manners?" Mama gave an unladylike sniff. "Say thank you to the young man, Patricia."

Patricia turned, fixing her enormous blue eyes on the young man. "Thank you," she whispered.

The young man froze. He stared at her for a long, long moment, and Seraphine saw his grey eyes fill with tears.

"What is it?" she asked. "What's the matter?"

The man said nothing. He just turned and disappeared into the crowd.

LENA FELT A PLEASANT NOTE OF SURPRISE RUN THROUGH her veins as she stepped into the shop, a basket over her arm. All week, she hadn't been able to stop thinking about the little girl with the blonde curls, and now she was right here in the shop, bouncing around in excitement and clapping her hands.

"There you are!" laughed Mrs. Weston, smiling as Lena came

inside. "I was just telling these two little customers of yours that you would be back soon."

"I just popped out for some bread," said Lena, smiling as she indicated the basket on her arm.

"Hooray! I'm so glad you're here!" The little blonde girl ran up to Lena, threw her arms around her knees and gave her a heart-wrenching smile. "I wanted you to help my mama with her hat."

Lena swallowed, a little disconcerted. The eyes gazing up at her now were the same ones that looked back at her in the mirror every morning.

"Well, I'm sure we can arrange that." She touched the little girl's cheek, frowning as she noticed a bruise forming there. "What happened to your face, darling?"

"Patty ran out onto the road while we were on our way here," said the older sister. Her solemn face wore a look of disapproval. "She almost got trampled by a runaway cart."

"It was very scary," said the little girl, widening her eyes.

"Luckily, a nice young man rescued her and saved the day," said their mother.

Lena looked up, meeting the lady's eyes for the first time. And there it was again – a shock rippling through her, a note of something familiar that she couldn't quite place. She paused, staring for a second, and she saw the lady do the same. Her face was so unfamiliar, yet there was something about her deep amber eyes that Lena was sure she'd seen before. Something strong tugged at her memories, and her thoughts were in turmoil.

"See, Mama?" said the older girl. "I told you she looked just like Patty."

The spell broke. The lady looked down at her daughter, laughing. "You're quite right, Seraphine. The resemblance is... striking." Her eyes wandered back up to Lena's.

Lena swallowed, trying to regain her equilibrium. "I'm glad to hear that you all got here in one piece," she said.

"Now show her," said Patty, tugging at Lena's skirt. "Show her the pretty green hat."

Lena had been keeping it just for them. As she lifted it down from the shelf, she tried to shake the strange feeling that looking at the lady had given her. Yet judging by the way that Seraphine's eyes were following her every movement, she wasn't the only one who felt that something uncanny had just happened.

❦

"I'll shut up the shop, Mrs. Weston," said Lena.

Mrs. Weston paused, looking up from where she was

frowning down at her ledger behind the counter. "Are you sure, darling?" she said.

"Of course," said Lena.

Mrs. Weston glanced at the grandfather clock in the corner. "It's still early," she said reluctantly.

"Nobody is going to come in now, ma'am," said Lena. "It's late on Christmas Eve. Everyone is going home to their families – as should you. I know that Tommy and his wife and children have come to visit you."

Mrs. Weston smiled at the mention of her grandchildren. Lena knew they meant the whole world to the old lady. "I suppose you're right," she said. "You can lock up early if you like, Lena."

Lena shrugged. "I don't mind. I sleep in the back room in any case, so it's no effort for me."

"You're a good girl." Mrs. Weston paused, touching Lena's cheek. "Merry Christmas, love. Are you sure you won't join us?"

Lena put on a smile. She knew the invitation was only given out of pity, and Lena simply couldn't make herself accept it. "No, no, I'm fine, ma'am. You have a merry Christmas now."

As the old lady bustled off, Lena leaned against the counter, deep in thought. It wasn't exactly a merry Christmas, although it was certainly better than the cold and lonely one that she'd spent in the basement of that single friendly house-keeper. Yet Christmas had never been the same. Not since Farley had left.

She wandered through the shop, straightening out the bunting, brushing her fingertips against the figures on the tree that she and Tommy had set up in the corner. Her heart went back to the last Christmas that she remembered being more or less happy: the one when she and Farley had sung together to the children. She had been so cold, so hungry and so afraid of Judas and Delilah. But the look in his deep grey eyes – it had meant everything. Pausing by the window, she leaned on the sill, her breath making a small white cloud on the glass.

"Where are you, Farley?" she whispered to the gathering dusk.

Was he out there somewhere? Was he still alive? Did he remember her?

Did he miss her?

Lena sighed. None of this was doing any good. It was time to lock the doors; no more customers would be coming in, not today. She grabbed a tinderbox from the counter and stepped out into the cool evening as the lamplighter strolled along the sidewalk, whistling "Silent Night" and leaving little puddles of light in his wake. Lena pulled the shutters of the big display window closed.

"Miss?"

Lena turned. It was Seraphine, the older of the two sisters, the one with the long black hair. She was staring up at Lena, and her expression had never been more solemn.

"Seraphine!" Lena forced a smile despite her melancholy heart. "What can I do to help you? Do you need another hat?"

Seraphine shook her head. Her eyes were fixed on Lena's, and there was something almost pleading in them. She took a deep breath, and Lena could see her shoulders shaking as she spoke.

"Once upon a time," she said, her words coming out on a cloud of curling steam, "there was a little bird who lived in a cosy nest in the woods."

Lena stopped. She held her breath, unable to move.

Seraphine took another breath and went on. "The little bird lived with his mama and papa and they loved each other very, *very* much." Her voice broke a little. "One day, the bird's mama and papa went out to find some seeds and berries for dinner."

Lena felt her hands shaking. She lifted them to her face, covering her mouth as tears filled her throat, her eyes, pouring out down her cheeks. She could remember those words. They rang true and steady through her heart, through her memories. Read out loud to her by a woman with deep amber eyes, and now echoed by a little girl as she continued to tell the story.

"When the wind stopped, the little bird was on the other side of the forest. He had never been so far away from his nest before, and he didn't know how to get back home." Seraphine bit her lip, and her eyes were filling with tears too. "He was so afraid," she whispered.

The tears were pouring freely down Lena's cheeks now, running between her fingers. As Seraphine told the story, she seemed to fade. The icy street, the years of hardship that separated them began to melt away, and Lena was a little girl again, giggling in Mama's lap. Listening to her favourite story.

"As the wolf came closer and closer, the little bird flapped and flapped his wings." Seraphine wiped at her tears. "And then, when the wolf was almost upon him, he jumped up – and he began to fly!"

Lena knew this part well. Seraphine told her how the little bird had flown, had seen his view of the world. "He spread out his wings and flew home in a jiffy," she murmured. "He settled back into his nest and said to himself..."

Lena couldn't help herself. She spoke the words alongside Seraphine. "The world is very beautiful," she choked out between her tears. "But flying is for going home."

Seraphine broke down, sobbing, tears cascading down her cheeks. She held out her arms and spoke a single word. "Lena?"

"It's me!" Lena ran the two steps to Seraphine and seized her in a heartfelt embrace. "It's me, Seraphine. It's me, Lena. It's me!"

Lena had never felt so many things at once. She couldn't put a name to all of the emotions coursing through her heart, so she didn't try; she just clung to her sister, crying her heart out as Seraphine pulled her closer.

"I can't believe it's you," Seraphine gasped. "I can't believe it's really you. They said you were dead."

"Dead?" cried Lena. "Who said that?"

"The police." Seraphine drew back, wiping at her tears. "Mama told me that they found your body in the river just a few months before I was born."

Lena shook her head. "But it wasn't me, Seraphine." She laughed, tears still streaming down her cheeks. "I'm here. It's me, Lena. I'm alive."

"Oh, Lena!" Seraphine gripped her hands, laughing through her tears. "Mama has always told Patty and me that we had an older sister – one who looked just like Patty, and that her name was Lena. We light a candle for you every single Christmas." Her voice broke. "And to think you've been alive all of these years."

"I thought I was forgotten," said Lena.

"Never! Mama and Papa would never," said Seraphine. "Even though they thought you were dead, they never stopped loving you, Lena." She stared up at her sister, her eyes fierce. "They would never let you go."

Lena had no words. She pulled Seraphine into her arms, feeling as though the scene could hardly be real. As if it wasn't her own life that could turn out this way. Seraphine pulled away, gripping Lena's hand. "Come on, Lena!" she said. "I have to take you home. Mama and Papa will be so happy!"

Lena stopped, overwhelmed. She swallowed hard. Had the little bird been almost as afraid to fly home as he had been of the woods? Would her family still want her after all these years? What would they think of the way she had become? She glanced at Seraphine's beautiful dress, then down at her own.

"Oh, Seraphine, I look terrible."

"Lena." Seraphine gripped her hands. "You are you. That's all they've been missing – for eleven years."

Lena nodded, swallowing hard. "Do you think they'll be glad to see me?"

"They'll be overjoyed to see you!" Seraphine hesitated, frowning. "Although it will be a terrible shock for Mama."

Lena thought of her mother's pale face. "Don't you think we should break it to her gently?" she asked. "What if you went home and spoke to Papa, and he told Mama?"

"Oh, Lena, I don't want to leave you here," said Seraphine.

"I'm safe here," Lena reassured her. "I'll be fine for one more night."

"All right." Seraphine nodded. "I think that would be best. Mama will be so happy. Everyone will be so happy." Her face split in a huge grin as she wiped away her tears. "I'm so glad that I've found you."

Lena squeezed her sister's hands. "Thank you for coming to find me," she said sincerely.

"I'll come and get you tomorrow morning. With a carriage!" Seraphine laughed. "I'll see you soon, Lena. This is going to be the best Christmas present ever."

"See you, Seraphine."

Lena watched as the little figure ran off down the sidewalk, her hair streaming out behind her like a shadow. Lena's legs felt shaky, and her breaths were quick and ragged with joy. Miss Weston had been right. Christmas was the time for miracles.

Yet as she stepped back into the shop, she couldn't help but feel that something was missing. She wished with all of her heart that she could tell Farley everything. That she could bring him home with her. That she could share her joy with him.

That she could share everything with him.

CHAPTER 16

The morning was so crisp and clear that Lena felt as though she'd been trapped on the inside of a diamond. Everything sparkled: the sunshine on the fallen snow, the brightness of the early sky, even the great shining palisades of the gates just ahead of her. She plunged her shaking hands into the pockets of her work-worn dress. They'd been trembling with cold when she'd first left the shop, but now they trembled for another reason.

Because Lena recognized the gates in front of her.

She paused, gazing up at them. She vaguely remembered the palisades, but each pillar of the gates was mounted by a stone horse's head, and those she remembered. The horses' mouths were wide open, their eyes frightened, and she remembered because they were the last thing she had seen the night Ella had dragged her out of her home.

Legs shaking, Lena stepped forward, reaching out to brush her fingers against the palisades. For four years, she had been living so close to her family. For eleven, she had been longing to see them again. Yet despite the impulse that had driven her from her bed early that morning and pushed her to look for the receipt that Mrs. Weston had written for them – the one with their address on it in her fine copperplate writing – now she began to wonder if she was really ready to meet them again.

If she would be everything they had hoped.

She peered through the palisades, and the lawn was familiar, too, even carpeted in thick white snow. The hedges lining the driveway had flitted past the window of the carriage so many times as they travelled to see friends, Lena safely cradled in Mama's lap. The bench by the wall of the house, where Sally used to sit while Lena played in the snow. The house's fine windows were all still behind closed curtains, but Lena knew somewhere in there was the nursery where Mama used to read to her, and it made her heart beat too fast.

Then, a footman stepped out of the house. Lena's breath caught as he opened the main doors and a little figure slipped out, black hair cascading down its back. Seraphine broke into a run when she spotted Lena at the gates. Feet crunching on the gravel, she hastened to Lena's side.

"Lena!" she gasped, her eyes shining. "I said I'd come to fetch you."

"And I believed you," said Lena, "but I just couldn't wait." She clutched at Seraphine's hands through the palisades. "Oh, Seraphine, I'm so afraid."

"You don't have to be afraid, silly," said Seraphine. She smiled, pulling at the big gates to get them open just enough for Lena to slip inside.

"How did they take it?" Lena asked. "Were they... upset?"

Seraphine grinned up at her and took her hand. "Well, Mama fainted. But when she came round, she was so happy. We're all happy, Lena. We're just so glad that you're home."

And in Lena's very bones, it felt like home too, as she walked up the long drive with her trembling hand in Seraphine's. She knew that her feet had crunched on this gravel before, that she had played on those lawns, slept in that mighty house, and she knew it in her soul—but her fluttering heart felt as though it might fly out of her chest with fear.

When they reached the main doors, the grizzled footman had tears soaking into the wrinkles on his cheeks and a huge grin on his face.

"Oh, Miss Lena, welcome home!" he said.

Lena didn't know him, but he must have known her; she managed to smile back and then they were walking into the entrance hall and Mama was there. Lena knew she'd seen her just a few days ago, yet she had just been a lady then. Now that she knew she was Mama, she remembered more. She remembered those soft hands tickling her tummy. She remembered those amber eyes, even though right now they were shining with tears, and the expression in them almost broke her. She froze, facing her mother across the marble surface of the newly polished floor.

Mama was standing with Papa's arm around her shoulders. They were both staring at her, and Lena didn't know their wrinkled faces, but she knew their shining eyes. She wanted nothing more than to run to them, but in her faded dress, the grandeur of the place rooted her to the spot.

"Mama, Papa," said Seraphine, beaming. "It's Lena. It's really her."

The silence stretched. Papa's lip was trembling, but Mama's face was as frozen as if she were a beautiful marble bust. Lena felt her heart drop into her shoes. What if they didn't want her? What if they sent her away? What if, seeing her in such a worn frock, they decided they were already happy with just their two perfect little girls?

Then Mama made a small, choking sound. She stepped forward, opening her arms. "Oh, my little bird," she croaked. "You came home at last."

"Flying is for coming home," Lena choked.

"Lena!" Mama gasped. "My darling, come to me."

Lena didn't need to be told twice. She rushed forward, flinging herself into her mother's arms, burying her face in Mama's fragrant neck. And then there were so many arms surrounding her – her mother's frail grasp, Patricia's thin arms around her legs, Seraphine clutching her waist, and the strong arms of her father surrounding them all. Holding his whole family back together.

FARLEY RESTED A HAND ON ANDREW'S FOREHEAD, TRYING to hold back a sigh. Despite the fierce, icy wind that buffeted their little hiding place in the alley, the boy was blazing hot to the touch. Farley looked into Andrew's terrified dark eyes and tried to scrape together a smile for him.

"Hush, Andy," he said, reaching into the leaky bucket of melted snow beside him. He grabbed the rag floating in the grubby water, wrung it out a little and patted Andrew's flushed cheeks with it. "I think it's coming down a little now. You'll be all right."

"I don't feel well," Andrew whispered through chapped, dry lips. He shivered and let out an awful cough – a harsh, bubbling sound. "My chest hurts."

"I know it does," said Farley. "Won't you try a little more of this soup?" he asked hopefully, touching the cup that he'd set carefully on a barrel beside them.

"No thank you," Andrew croaked. "I – I'm not hungry." He gave a sigh that was half cough, half groan. "Why am I not hungry? I'm always hungry."

"It's just the fever, Andy," said Farley, trying to swallow the fear boiling in his gut. "You'll be hungry again when it breaks, and then the soup will be right here waiting for you, all right?"

Andrew gave another cough. "You can have the soup," he whispered.

"No, no. You'll need it when you're getting better," said Farley.

"Will I get better?" Andrew asked. His eyes were hollow as he stared into Farley's face.

"Yes, you will," said Farley firmly. He ran the damp cloth down the dry, hot skin of Andrew's arms. "I know you will, because we're going to the country."

"The country?" Andrew's eyes widened. "How?"

"I've found some money," said Farley, not wanting to tell Andrew he'd stolen the shilling in his back pocket. He knew it was wrong, but what else could he do? "We're going to buy a train ticket and go out to the country and make our fortunes. And then the fresh air will make you all better."

Andrew's eyes were troubled. He gripped Farley's hand. "But what about Lena?"

Every time he heard her name out loud, it felt like a knife cutting deeply into Farley's heart. He swallowed hard, trying his best to hold back his tears. "Andy, I can't let you..." He paused, not wanting to say the word *die* out loud. "I can't let you be this sick just because I want to find her," he said gently.

"But you miss her, Farley. And you said she's still out there," said Andrew. "Do you think she's gone?"

"No," said Farley firmly. "I'll never believe that my Lena is gone. But I do know that if she were here, she would be telling me to take care of you." He closed his eyes, a smile stealing over him as he pictured her standing there with those deep, compassionate blue eyes. "She would tell me to go."

"We'll come back for her," said Andrew, but Farley could see the relief in his face. "We'll make our fortunes out there in the country, and then we'll come back and find Lena, I know we will."

Farley forced a smile. "So do I," he said. "Now, get some sleep."

It was only when the sickly little boy had descended into a restless slumber that Farley drew his knees up to his chest like a child, curled himself up and allowed the tears to overwhelm him.

LENA COULD HARDLY BELIEVE THAT SO MUCH COULD change in a matter of a single day and night.

She walked down the stairs from her luxurious room slowly, enjoying the feeling of the soft fabric of her brand-new dress caressing her skin as she walked. It made a beautiful, rustling sound, the rich sapphire-blue silk — the same shade as her eyes, she knew, from looking into the mirror — spilling down each step as she moved. Her curls were clean and had been neatly combed out; now they hung in a profusion of ringlets the colour of sunshine, tumbling around her neck and shoulders, their touch feather soft.

She reached up to her neck as she moved, touching the bejeweled necklace that hung there. She hadn't wanted to wear the necklace at first, but when Seraphine told her that Mama had bought it for her to wear as a young woman when she was just a little baby, she knew that she had to. The glittering surface of the sapphire set in gold was enchanting, scattering the light within.

"Oh, Lena!" cried Patricia's little voice. "You look like — like a princess."

Lena looked up. Her entire family was waiting at the bottom of the stairs for her. Patricia looked enchanted, her little hands clasped under her chin; Papa seemed to be three inches taller than he was yesterday, and Mama's eyes were raw from crying, but she knew that these were tears of joy.

"You're wearing the jewels that I bought you when you were just a baby," Mama gasped. "I put them away. I thought you'd never..." She beamed through her tears. "Oh, what a beautiful Christmas!"

Lena spotted Seraphine standing just behind them and shot her a grateful smile. "Thank you, Mama," she said. "It's just beautiful."

"You're just beautiful, my Lena," said Papa. He took her hand and kissed her delicately on the cheek. "Now come, my lovely daughter." He gave a booming belly-laugh. "Let's have a Christmas lunch worthy of all the lunches you've missed out on over the past eleven years!"

Lena allowed Papa to lead her into the beautiful dining hall. A glittering crystal chandelier hung from the ceiling, scattering light everywhere just like the heart of the sapphire resting on Lena's bosom. The table was set in only the finest silver, with candlesticks casting a gentle golden glow over the delicate china plates. The tablecloth was starched perfectly pure white, its edges elegantly embroidered in flowing figures of gold and silver. Papa pulled out Lena's chair for her, and she sat down, suppressing a giggle. It all just seemed so absurd, so surreal that this beauty and bounty could really be hers.

"Are you going to tell us all about your adventures, Lena?" asked Patricia, sitting down beside her.

"Patty, darling, Lena doesn't have to tell us right now," said Papa gently. "Lena had a very difficult time while she was gone."

"I – I would like to share my story, Papa, by your leave," said Lena quietly. "So much has happened that I want you all to know." She looked at Mama's teary eyes. "If you don't mind."

"Oh, darling!" Mama reached over the table to grip Lena's hand. "I want to hear everything."

As the appetizers arrived, Lena was grateful that Mrs. Weston had given her enough to eat. Otherwise, she knew that she would have disgraced herself if she'd had to survive on the meagre fare that Judas and Delilah provided all these years. She began to tell them all about what had happened to her. When she told her family that it was Ella who had taken her, Papa's face turned purest white. He shot an apologetic look at the butler, who stood attentively by the door.

"You tried to warn me, Godfrey," he said. "You told me not to trust her." He shook his head. "I was suspicious ever since she ran away that Christmas, but now I know for sure."

Godfrey looked deeply angered himself. "If I could get my hands on that girl," he growled. Then, remembering his manners, he cleared his throat. "Pardon me, sir."

Lena went on, telling them about Judas and Delilah and how they forced her to beg and then to teach the other children to beg. She told them about Emily. Mama and Papa exchanged glances, their faces filled with dismay.

"We read about it in the paper," said Mama. "Oh, Lena, if we had known..."

"You didn't know, Mama," said Lena. She rested her hand over Mama's. "You thought I was gone. It's not your fault."

"How did you survive?" asked Seraphine, her eyes round.

"Well, I went from one house to the other, knocking on the doors and asking for work or help, all that Christmas Eve," said Lena. "It was bitterly cold."

"I remember," said Papa quietly. He leaned forward, the roast goose on his plate forgotten. "You couldn't have survived outside, Lena."

"I didn't have to. There was just one housekeeper who let me in," said Lena. "She risked her job to give me somewhere safe to sleep that night. It could only be for one night, but it was the coldest night of the year – she saved my life with that small piece of kindness."

"I wish we could find her and thank her," said Mama. "What happened after that?"

"Well, I had to leave the next morning, so I went from door to door again asking for work," said Lena. "I had to sleep in doorways or alleys for a few days, but finally, I came to Mrs. Weston's hat shop." She smiled. "And Mrs. Weston saved me.

I've been there for four years, and she cares for me like her own daughter."

"She'll be richly rewarded," said Papa with enthusiasm. "I'll see to it that she has everything she needs as she gets older."

"Oh, thank you, Papa." Lena gripped his hand. "Mrs. Weston was so terribly good to me. And in all those years, there were only three people who were ever really good to me. Mrs. Weston and the kind housekeeper who let me stay that Christmas night…" She paused, and the little ache in her heart that had been throbbing consistently for five years intensified. "And Farley," she murmured.

"Who's Farley?" asked Patricia.

"He was one of the children in the house with Judas and Delilah," said Lena. "He was my only friend. He was always there for me, and he always looked after me. I… I don't think I would have survived those first years without him." She looked down. "I don't think I could have made it through all those dark nights without the hope that I would find him again someday." Her eyes blurred with tears. "Farley got me through it all, even when he wasn't with me."

"What happened to him?" asked Mama.

"He went to rob a townhouse one night – Judas and Delilah forced him." Lena looked up, wiping at her tears. "And he just never came back. I don't know what happened to him, but

Papa..." She turned her eyes on her father, pleading. "Oh, Papa, do you think we could find out?"

Papa gave a fierce nod. "Lena, my darling, for what this Farley has done for you, I will move heaven and earth to find him," he said. "He helped to bring you home safely to me, and I could never ask for more." He took her hand and kissed her fingers. "We'll find him somehow. I'll do everything in my power – I promise."

"But how?" asked Lena. "I've searched so hard for so long."

"Well, what does he look like?" asked Seraphine sensibly. "Do you remember?"

Lena smiled despite her tears. "How could I ever forget?" she said. "He has beautiful, curly hair – it was always a little shaggy because Judas would cut it with a kitchen knife." She touched her own curls. "And it's the colour of wheat waiting for the harvest. He's tall, too, and lanky when I last saw him, but he must have been only thirteen or fourteen then."

"That's good, Lena," said Papa encouragingly. "Do you remember anything else?"

"He has soft grey eyes – they look like a gentle grey mist," said Lena. "Pale and beautiful. And he has a scar just here." She drew a finger down her cheek.

Seraphine, Patricia, and Mama were staring at her. The colour was draining from Mama's face, and Patricia's mouth was curling into a smile.

"What is it?" asked Lena. Her heart thumped. "Why are you so pale, Mama?"

"Oh, Lena!" said Patricia. "We saw him. We met him!"

"We can't be sure it was him," said Seraphine.

"But it must be, Sera," said Patricia. "He had the same hair and eyes, and the same scar, and he was also so very tall."

"Where did you see him?" Lena cried.

Mama's eyes were full of tears again. "Lena, he saved your sister's life," she said.

"What?" Lena's heart was pounding. "Wait – when you told me that Patricia nearly got run over and someone saved her..."

"It was him, Lena," said Mama, laughing and crying. "It was Farley."

"Then I owe two daughters to this young man," said Papa. "And I am going to start looking for him."

Lena was overcome. She buried her face in her hands, gratitude and hope flooding through her soul. She had already gained her whole family this Christmas.

The knowledge that Farley was out there – alive and whole and himself – was almost more than she could bear.

CHAPTER 17

Andrew's weight dragged at Farley's hips and shoulders. He hefted the boy a little higher on his back, stifling a groan as his aching body struggled with the extra weight. He paused a moment for breath, listening to the huff of steam and the hiss of the engine as he tried to push through the crowd gathered by the train station.

"I can walk, Farley," Andrew offered.

It was tempting to put him down, but Farley knew by the way that Andrew was leaning his head against Farley's shoulder that the little boy still felt weak even though the fever had broken two days before, on Christmas Day. He shook his head, trying to sound cheerful even though he felt as though both of his boots were made of lead.

"It's all right, Andy," he said. "Rest up – we're almost on the train."

"Is it very far to the country?" asked Andrew.

"I don't know," Farley admitted. "I've never been there before. But we'll sit in the lovely train, and you can have a sleep, all right? It's going to be your first time on a train, Andy. Aren't you excited?"

Andrew tried to giggle, then coughed instead. "I am excited," he said valiantly.

Farley knew Andrew was trying to make him feel better. He hoped the little boy hadn't woken up to see Farley crying to himself every night since he'd decided to take Andrew out to the countryside. He didn't want Andrew to know how he really felt about leaving behind the city that had chewed him up and spat him out, the city that nonetheless still had the most priceless jewel in the world hidden somewhere in its grotesque and diseased bowels.

"What kind of jobs are we going to get?" Andrew asked.

"Well, hopefully you won't need one," said Farley. He took out the shilling, keeping Andrew safely on his back, and went over to the ticket office. "Maybe I can be a groom or a cowhand."

"I like horses," said Andrew dreamily. "Being a groom sounds like fun."

"Maybe when you're older," said Farley. He smiled at the man in the ticket office, who glared at him with disdain as if he knew how Farley had come by that shilling. With a scowl, he gave him two tickets. Farley gripped them tightly, knowing his dirty hands were smearing the paper.

A pang of guilt ran through him as he headed toward the train. He had pickpocketed that money, and he knew it was wrong. The guilt turned to nervousness as he saw a policeman give him a wary look as he crossed the platform toward the train. Did the copper know somehow? What was he going to do if they tried to arrest him? What would happen to Andrew?

But the policeman didn't move, and Farley had almost made it across the platform. He let out a breath of relief, holding out his ticket to the conductor. The tickets were punched, and Farley paused a foot from the door of the train. The crowd murmured angrily behind him, wanting to push into the train, but he couldn't help it. He looked back, his eyes scanning the crowd one last time, the way he had scanned every crowd ever since escaping from the workhouse.

"Oh, Lena," he whispered. "If you're going to appear, please, you have to do it now."

But there was no Lena. No shining blue eyes. No bouncing golden curls. Farley turned, his heart leaden, and stepped toward the train.

"Hey!" a voice rang out across the platform. It was masculine, commanding, used to being obeyed. "Hey, you!"

Farley instinctively cringed. He glanced back, wondering who had attracted so much anger, and saw a stocky man with piercing blue eyes pushing through the crowd. Those eyes were fixed on Farley. "You!" the man hollered.

"What does he want?" cried Andrew, his voice high with fear.

Farley froze, looking wildly around for a way to run. The man he'd pickpocketed had been muffled up in coat and scarf – it could easily be the one pushing his way across the platform now. It seemed absurd that a rich man would kick up such a fuss over a shilling, but here he was now, and Farley needed to get away, to get Andrew to safety. He spotted an opening in the crowd and lunged—

"Stop!" yelled the man. "Farley! Stop!"

Farley froze. As the crowd surged around him, he turned back, fear and confusion filling his heart. How did the man know his name?

The train whistled impatiently, but the man had made it to Farley's side. He shoved through the crowd and stared at him breathlessly, his eyes dwelling for a minute on the scar that marked Farley's cheek. His mouth opened, and Farley braced himself for the accusation.

Instead, his words were breathy, unbelieving. "It really is you."

The policeman appeared behind the man, and Farley instinctively tensed. But instead of striding forward to clap the handcuffs on him, the copper merely nodded. "Is this the man you were looking for, sir?" he asked the blue-eyed man.

The man nodded. "Yes, yes – thank you very much, my good man," he said. "I believe it is." He stepped forward. "Farley, is it you?"

Farley swallowed. "How do you know my name?"

"Oh, my dear boy." The man smiled. To Farley's shock, tears were glittering in his eyes. "I have heard it over and over in the past few days, spoken with such love and admiration that I could hardly believe you were even real."

"I don't understand," said Farley.

The man reached out a hand. Farley flinched for a moment, then tentatively took it.

"Farley, I owe you the lives of two of my beautiful daughters," said the man.

"What do you mean?" asked Farley.

"My dear boy." The man beamed through his emotions. "I'm Lena Phillips's father."

A bolt of lightning may as well have shot down from the sky and struck through Farley's body, lancing in an arc of unstoppable electricity all the way from the top of his head down through his bare feet. He could barely breathe, barely stand. He slowly lowered Andrew to the ground, terrified he would drop him.

"Lena?" he croaked. "Is she – is she all right?"

"I know you must know her from the look on your face." Lena's father laughed. "Yes, dear boy, she's fine, she's completely fine. She's at home right now, safe with her mother and sisters at last."

"Lena found you again?" Farley wasn't sure if he was laughing or crying. "The little bird did fly home in the end?"

"Yes, she did," said the man. "And ever since she got home, she's done nothing except plead with me to find you. She misses you. She hasn't given up on you, Farley, just as it appears you never gave up on her." Mr. Phillips practically wrung Farley's hand. "And that hope is what got her through eleven years of being lost to us."

"May – may I see her?" Farley gasped.

"Of course, you may. That's why I came to find you." Mr. Phillips put a fatherly arm around Farley's shoulders, only shuddering slightly at the dirt and lice on his clothes. "I came to repay you for saving my little Patricia from a runaway cart and my beautiful Lena from years of hardship."

"Patricia – oh!" Farley remembered. "She looks so much like Lena..."

"She does. And she recognised you. That's how we found you, with the help of the police." Mr. Phillips laughed. "Now tell me, Farley, I need to know just one thing from you. What do you need? What can I give you?" He smiled tearfully. "Anything, my boy. Anything – for what you did for my daughters. I would give you the very clothes off my back."

Farley turned, reaching for Andrew's hand. "Sir, please, if you could just help this little boy." He pulled Andrew into his shaking arms again, settling him on his hip. "He has no one but me."

Mr. Phillips laid a hand on Andrew's cheek, pity creeping into his eyes. "Of course," he said warmly. "I have a flat that has been empty for a few weeks in town. It will be yours – both of yours. And I will see to it that you have all that you need, that you learn a trade to support yourself."

Farley could hardly believe his ears. He felt the hot tears prickling behind his eyes. "Mr. Phillips, sir, I can't..."

"Hush now, my boy." Mr. Phillips gripped his hand. "I don't want to hear it. You're coming with me, and then you're going to have a good bath and get dressed in proper clothes while I send a messenger to fetch Lena in the carriage." His eyes were damp, but they shone. "She can't wait to see you again."

❦

LENA KNEW THAT SHE WOULD HAVE TO LEARN TO BE A LADY, but that learning would have to come tomorrow, because right now she was going to run. She half fell out of the carriage, and the elderly footman had to dive to steady her as she nearly tripped on the curb.

"Easy there, miss!" he cried.

"Oh, Frank, I'm just so excited!" she gasped.

Frank laughed. "There – the red door," he said. "He's right through there, waiting for you."

"Thank you!" Lena cried. She threw her arms around Frank's neck and gave him a smacking kiss on the cheek, and then she ran. Her hoop skirt bounced, her corset pinching at her chest, but she didn't care. All she knew was that Farley was behind that door. She bounded up the steps in one great leap, shoved the door open, crashed down the passageway and ended up in a little sitting room.

Papa was there, laughing at her expression. She grabbed his arms. "Oh, Papa, where is he?"

"He's just getting dressed. He'll be here in a moment."

"Papa, thank you, thank you!" Lena hugged him with all of her strength. "Oh, thank you!"

Papa kissed her cheek. "Anything for you, darling."

"And Andrew?" Lena asked. "Is he all right?"

"He will be. The physician is tending to him," said Papa tenderly, laying a hand on her shoulder.

Lena opened her mouth to thank him again, and then she heard his voice again for the first time in five years.

"Lena?"

She turned. Farley was standing there, neatly dressed in a grey suit the same colour as his eyes, but he was her same Farley. And he was holding out his arms to her, and Lena knew that Mrs. Weston had been right. Christmas was the time of miracles. She flew to him. Flew into his embrace.

Flew home.

CHAPTER 18

One Year Later

LENA KNEW THE NOTES OF "JOY TO THE WORLD" WELL enough by now that her fingers moved across the pianoforte's keys all by themselves as she raised her voice to join the sweet music that rose up from the beloved instrument. How she loved the song, and how grateful she was for the music lessons her father had provided for her. The beautiful old Christmas hymn filled the room, perfecting the merry atmosphere.

Every surface was hung with holly and mistletoe; a great log burned brightly in the fireplace, and the tree in the centre of the room was beautifully adorned with every decoration. Presents wrapped in brown paper and decorated with ribbons were tucked neatly at the foot of the tree, and the blazing golden star at its head almost touched the chandelier.

But it wasn't the decorations or the tree or the presents or even the music that made the room the happiest place Lena had ever been. It was the people. Andrew and Patricia, partners in crime, sat side by side with chocolate smeared over their faces as they tried to sing along with their mouths full of stolen goodies. Ever prim and proper, Seraphine was sitting with her legs crossed demurely, her pure and piercing voice rising up to join with Lena's as seamlessly as they had joined in friendship. Mama, her cheeks glowing with health once more, sat close to Papa on the settee. Mrs. Weston had had a little too much of the eggnog, but her face was alight with joy, and she was joining in the hymn as well as she could.

And Farley, at the end of the room, perched on the edge of the armchair, was singing with his eyes closed. His whole heart poured out into the lyrics, just as Lena remembered it doing when they were two starving children trying to keep their roommates' spirits up. She gazed at him, her heart feeling like it might explode, so full of joy it was. This room held everything she'd ever wanted, more than she'd ever dared to hope for.

The song came to an end, and Lena sat back, breathless, as the whole room burst into applause.

"Oh, Lena, you've gotten so good at this," cried Mrs. Weston.

"Thank you." Lena laughed. "I've had plenty of practice."

"Now, why don't you play something for us, Farley dear?" asked Mama, smiling over at Farley. "You are so lovely on the harmonica."

Farley rose, inclining his head. Lena's heart beat even faster; in just a year, her beloved street urchin had been transformed into a consummate gentleman.

"By your leave, Mrs. Phillips, I won't play right now," he said, "but I do have something to say." He stepped over to the piano, standing beside Lena, and held out a hand. She got up, taking it.

"What is it, love?" she asked.

Farley cleared his throat, turning to the rest of the family. "A year ago today, I was desperate," he said. "I was going to leave London and seek a better life for myself and Andrew, but I had stopped believing there was a better life out there. That is, until you came to find me, Mr. Phillips." He nodded at Papa. "Because you asked him to, my darling." He kissed Lena's cheek. "You say you can never repay me, but I believe you have repaid me a thousand-fold. You have given Andrew and me a place to lay our heads and you made sure that Andrew was healthy, and you have given me the opportunity to study – and, God willing, to become a doctor one day."

"You'll be a fine doctor, Farley," said Papa. Lena thought she saw something secret and mischievous dancing in her father's eyes.

"But as thankful as I am for my studies, Mr. Phillips, there's one thing you've given me that I'm far more thankful for." He turned to Lena, and his grey eyes were shining with such love that they looked silver. "The opportunity to do this." He kissed her forehead, and then sank swiftly to one knee, lifting a little red box out of his pocket.

Lena clapped her hand over her mouth. She stared, mute, as Farley opened the box and she saw the glitter of a diamond on the velvet inside.

"Lena Phillips," said Farley, solemnly. "Would you do me the honour of becoming my wife?"

Lena stared at him, and then at her family, and then up at the great Christmas tree, and she could barely contain the emotion flooding through her soul. One thing she knew for sure: there was no time of the year quite like Christmas.

She gazed down at Farley. There could only ever have been one answer. She whispered it to the world and whispered joy into her future.

"Yes, Farley. Yes."

The End

CONTINUE READING...

Thank you for reading *A Desolate Christmas!* **Are you wondering what to read next?** Why not read ***The Forsaken Maid's Secret?* Here's a sneak peek for you:**

Bincy clung to her mother's hand as they moved through the street. Mama was walking quickly today; her scarf was pulled tightly around her throat, her hat low over her eyes, and Bincy had to hurry to keep up. Running made her chest burn a little, but she knew Mama had a reason for being in a hurry.

"Where are we going, Mama?" she asked, pausing to cough.

Mama looked down at her. Her mother's eyes had been blue once, but the pressure of hardship seemed to have squeezed the color out of them; now they were watery and gray, just like the weather.

"Just to buy something for dinner," she said, with a quick smile.

"Dinner?" Bincy's heart leapt. "Oh, that'll be nice, Mama. I'm so hungry."

"I know you are, darling." Mama sighed. She gave Bincy's arm a little tug. "You and all four of your siblings, just like you've been for the seven months since your papa..." She stopped.

"Why did he leave?" asked Bincy. "Where did he go?"

"I've told you and told you. Where he went, I don't know," said Mama shortly. "I don't want to know, either. And as for why he left, I suppose we were just one problem too many for him." Her voice was bitter.

Bincy held Mama's hand more tightly. "I'm sorry I made you sad."

"It's not your fault," said Mama with a long sigh.

"I'm not gonna think about him," said Bincy, trying to make her mother feel better. "Let's think about the nice dinner we're going to have soon. We're going to all sit and eat together, and it's going to be nice. We haven't had anything all day, but now we're all going to go to bed with full tummies."

To Bincy's surprise, a tear sneaked out of the corner of Mama's eye. She dashed it away quickly, but Bincy had seen it. "Why are you crying?" she asked, scared. The last time Mama had cried had been when Bincy's little brother, Jack, had died in the night. "Is someone dead?"

"No, no, my darling. Nothing like that," said Mama. "Hush now. Just hush and walk with me, there's a good girl."

Bincy obeyed, holding Mama's hand as they reached the outskirts of the slum where they lived. Everyone in the area had grown used to the smell; it was a strangely dynamic thing, changing every morning and every time the wind blew, alternately bringing whiffs in from the rotting Thames or the deep reek from the factories that bordered one side of the slum.

The streets themselves had their own special smell, too. There was no horse manure in the street; instead, the animal excrement that lay there was of a more noxious nature, mingled with the rotting carcasses of rats and mice. There was no rotten food lying in the streets, either. Someone would have picked it up and devoured it, regardless of how bad it was. Bincy knew this because there had been days when she would happily have been that someone.

But today wasn't going to be one of those days. They were going to buy dinner, Mama had said. They left the slum behind and headed toward the marketplace. Bincy managed a skip or two as she kept pace with her mother.

The marketplace was bustling. Bincy stuck close to Mama's skirt as they wove their way through the crush of bodies, staring around wide-eyed at the open square and the shops that lined it. There was a grocer, and a baker, and even a seamstress. Bincy liked the bright colors of the dresses proudly displayed in the window. She knew better than to ask Mama if she could have one, though. Instead, she decided to set her hopes on the fragrant loaves of fresh bread that stood stacked in golden rows in front of the bakery.

"Are we going to get one of those, Mama?" she asked.

Mama seemed distracted. "Hmm? What?"

Visit Here to Continue Reading:'

http://www.ticahousepublishing.com/victorian-romance.html

THANKS FOR READING

If you **love Victorian Romance, Visit Here**

https://victorian.subscribemenow.com/

to hear about all **New Faye Godwin Romance Releases! I will let you know as soon as they become available!**

Thank you, Friends! If you enjoyed *A Desolate Christmas!* would you kindly take a couple minutes to leave a positive review on Amazon? It only takes a moment, and positive reviews truly make a difference. Thank you so much! I appreciate it!

Much love,

Faye Godwin

MORE FAYE GODWIN VICTORIAN ROMANCES!

We love rich, dramatic Victorian Romances and have a library of Faye Godwin titles just for you! (Remember that ALL of Faye's Victorian titles can be downloaded FREE with Kindle Unlimited!)

VISIT HERE to discover Faye's Complete Collection of Victorian Romance:

https://ticahousepublishing.com/victorian-romance.html

ABOUT THE AUTHOR

Faye Godwin has been fascinated with Victorian Romance since she was a teen. After reading every Victorian Romance in her public library, she decided to start writing them herself —which she's been doing ever since. Faye lives with her husband and young son in England. She loves to travel throughout her country, dreaming up new plots for her romances. She's delighted to join the Tica House Publishing family and looks forward to getting to know her readers.

contact@ticahousepublishing.com

Printed in Great
Britain
by Amazon